I0639539

Augustin Daly, Susanna Centlivre, Mrs. Hannah Cowley

**Two Old Comedies**

The Belle's Stratagem - by Mrs. Cowley - and The Wonder - by Mrs.

Centlivre - reduced and re-arranged by Augustin Daly for production at

Daly's Theatre

Augustin Daly, Susanna Centlivre, Mrs. Hannah Cowley

**Two Old Comedies**
*The Belle's Stratagem - by Mrs. Cowley - and The Wonder - by Mrs. Centlivre - reduced and re-arranged by Augustin Daly for production at Daly's Theatre*

ISBN/EAN: 9783337191337

Printed in Europe, USA, Canada, Australia, Japan

Cover: Foto ©Andreas Hilbeck / pixelio.de

More available books at **www.hansebooks.com**

# TWO
# OLD COMEDIES

## THE BELLE'S STRATAGEM

### AND

## THE WONDER

*REDUCED AND RE-ARRANGED BY*

AUGUSTIN DALY

For Production at Daly's Theatre
During the Season 1893-94

PRIVATELY PRINTED
FROM THE PROMPT BOOKS OF DALY'S THEATRE
1893

# The Wonder and The Belle's Stratagem.

---

## A PREFACE.

### By WILLIAM WINTER.

### I.

THE note that is always audible in the old English comedies is the note of gallantry. The predominant impulse that animates their people is the impulse of desire. The figures that glisten and sparkle through their flowery and fragrant labyrinths of artifice, equivoque, raillery, frolic, and intrigue are the representative figures of languishing allurement, tantalizing witchery, gleeful mischief, and audacious and exultant animal life. In almost every one of them there is an enchanting maid or a superb widow, to be pursued and captured by a potential rake whom marriage will reform, or there is a wild and reckless cavalier, whom the omnipotent charms of awful and irresistible beauty are finally to invest with the rosy curb of the matrimonial yoke. Ardent man nimbly careers after enticing woman, and lovely and capricious woman exerts all her arts, either to allure or elude her follower, or discomfit her rival, or subdue her captor, or augment her triumphs. The time is always mating time, and the sole question is the question whether courtship will prosper and love prevail. Some of those old plays are grossly carnal and vulgar. Some of them are only coarse. Many of them are artificial and brittle. All of them burn with the fire of pleasure and palpitate with the warmth of physical enjoyment—

"The glow of young desire and purple light of love."

It would be easy to go into hysterics of disapprobation of their frequent immorality. Macaulay led the way in that. Vile enough some of them are, in the pages of such writers as Etherege and Sedley and Dryden and Aphra Behn. Yet even at their worst they are better than modern French plays relative to amorous intrigue and matrimonial infi-

3

delity—for they are only downright vulgar ; they are not sophistical, insidious, deceitfully humanitarian, and sentimentally corrupt. They do not instil depravity of principle, nor invent fine names for bad deeds, nor extenuate wrong-doing, nor celebrate incontinence, nor hover voluptuously about vice, nor revel in the analysis of morbid passion and hideous crime. Pleasure and mirth are at once their impulse and their signification. Besides, it is to be considered as a final reflection that the best of them are inoffensive, and that the worst of them do not survive. Our British ancestors liked animal mirth. The modern audience, if not more refined, is more fastidious.

One of the best of the representative old comedies—not as literature, but as a play to be acted—is " The Wonder," written by Mrs. Centlivre in the distant days of Queen Anne ; and a signal denotement of the vital practical merit of that piece is the fact that although it was produced one hundred and eighty years ago it is not discarded yet. In " The Wonder " the scheme is one of entanglement and cross-purposes. *Donna Violante* is dearly loved by *Don Felix*, and she dearly loves him in return. A serious passion, therefore, is the basis of the structure and the impulse of the movement. Furthermore, that passion is environed from the outset with serious difficulty. *Donna Violante* has been destined by her father, *Don Pedro*, for a convent—and *Don Pedro* is an imperious, irascible, and formidable old gentleman, whose purpose will not easily be defeated. *Don Felix*, accordingly, can only win his mistress by baffling her vigilant and expeditious sire. That situation is still further complicated from the fact that *Don Felix* has seriously wounded an antagonist in a duel ; has been obliged to fly from justice, in the city of Lisbon ; and has returned to that city in secrecy, but must not show himself for fear of arrest. *Donna Violante*, meantime, has given shelter to her fugitive friend, *Donna Isabella*, the sister of *Don Felix*, whose father, *Don Lopez*, would force her to a hateful marriage with a rich dotard. *Donna Isabella*, leaping from her window, has fallen into the arms of *Colonel Britton*—a most ardent military gentleman from England—and *Colonel Britton*, conveying her into the nearest accessible house, has brought her into the dwelling of *Donna Violante ;* and about that dwelling *Colonel Britton* proceeds to haunt. The secret to be preserved is the secret of *Donna Isabella's* identity. That secret is faithfully kept by *Donna Violante*, even at the peril of her reputation and her happiness, and under the stress of serious trials ; and " the wonder " is that a woman should keep a secret at all ! The peculiar felicity of the comedy is that of invention. Through scene after scene the jealousy of the fiery *Don Felix* is piqued by the subterfuges to which *Donna Violante* is unavoidably compelled, and also by suspicious complications resultant on the amorous enterprise of the restless and roving *Colonel Britton*. The clandestine mischief of *Lissardo*, servant to *Don Felix*, and of *Flora*, servant to *Donna Violante*,

tends still further to embroil those impetuous lovers, and at once to pro-
mote comic confusion and a sparkling vicissitude of merry and ludicrous
incident. The concealment of *Flora* in the apartments of *Don Felix* is
most adroitly contrived to cover him with confusion in the eyes of his
mistress. The great fertility of resource displayed by *Donna Violante*
stimulates continual mirth. *Lissardo*, loving *Flora*, and beloved by her,
but blandly promoting a wrangle for his favor between *Flora* and *Inis*,
provides a most amusing episode. The blended craft and simplicity of
*Gibby*, the Scotch servant of *Colonel Britton*, affords at once a droll sketch
of character and a prolific source of comic mischance and bewilderment.
The fruitless sapience of the self-complacent fathers—whose irrational
intents are agreeably defeated by the dexterity of youth and love—is
made an additional element in the general result of humor and happiness.
Mrs. Centlivre's style was never brilliant; she was not a good writer;
but she possessed the art of dramatic construction, and "The Wonder"
is a felicitous example of it.

Susanna Freeman (Mrs. Centlivre) was born in Ireland, in or about
1680. Her parents were English—her father being a native of Lincoln-
shire and her mother a native of Norfolk. She appears to have had an
unfortunate and unhappy childhood. While yet in her teens she was
wedded to a youth named Fox, who died a few months after marriage,
and she then became the wife of a gentleman named Carrol, an officer in
the British army, who presently was killed in a duel. She then became
a writer, under the name of Carrol, and produced a tragedy called "The
Perjured Husband, or Adventures of Venice," and also she went upon
the stage as an actress. In the latter vocation she did not succeed, but
while acting at Windsor, in Lee's tragedy of "The Rival Queens," she
bewitched the fancy of Mr. Joseph Centlivre, then cook to the Queen, and
by him she was wooed and won. In that marriage she was happy, and
for many years she enjoyed the society of London wits and busied herself
pleasantly in the composition and production of her plays. Steele, Rowe,
and Farquhar were among her friends. She had a pleasant home in
Spring Gardens, near Charing Cross, now the centre of activity in London, but in Queen Anne's day a rural retreat. In that home she died,
on December 1, 1723, and she was buried in the vaults beneath the
neighboring church of St. Martin-in-the-Fields. Her works were published, in three volumes, in 1761. She was essentially a writer for the
stage and not for the library. Her pieces are to be acted, not read.
They are noted for plenteous vicissitude of plot and for incident and
character, but they are neither trenchant in wit nor felicitous in language. The best of them are "The Wonder," "The Busybody," and
"A Bold Stroke for a Wife." Those comedies, when represented, move
with more expedition than is provided by the comedies of Congreve,
with their elaborate and perfect characterization and their beautifully

polished English ; but Congreve was vastly the superior writer and the greater mind.

Mrs. Centlivre wrote the following pieces : " The Perjured Husband," tragedy, 1701 ; " Love's Contrivance," comedy, 1703 ; " The Beau's Duel, or A Soldier for the Ladies," comedy, 1703 ; " The Stolen Heiress, or Salamanca Doctor Outwitted," comedy, 1704; " The Gamester," comedy, 1705 ; " The Basset Table," comedy, 1706 ; " Love at a Venture," comedy, 1706 ; " The Platonic Lady," comedy, 1707 ; " The Busybody," comedy, 1708 ; " The Man Bewitched, or The Devil to Do About Her," comedy, 1710 ; " Bickerstaff's Wedding, or Work for the Upholders "— also recorded as " A Bickerstaff's Burying "—farce, about 1710 ; " Marplot " (second part of the " Busybody "), comedy, 1711 ; " The Perplexed Lovers," comedy, 1712 ; " The Wonder—a Woman Keeps a Secret," comedy, 1714 ; " The Gotham Election," farce, 1715 ; " A Wife Well Managed," farce, 1715 ; " The Cruel Gift," tragedy, 1717 ; " A Bold Stroke for a Wife," comedy, 1718 ; " The Artifice," comedy, 1721.

Mrs. Centlivre may not have been much influenced by her brilliant contemporaries,* Congreve [1672–1729] and Farquhar [1678–1707]. Congreve's best works, however, were published before she began as an author [1701] ; all Farquhar's plays appeared between 1699 and 1707 ; and the same actors who performed in Farquhar's comedies performed also in hers. She certainly was acquainted with the dramatic writings of Aphra Behn [1642–1689], whose plays had not, in her time, lost their vogue, and to whose sceptre she succeeded, though inferior to that eccentric author, alike in genius and in the wanton abuse of it.

The comedy of " The Wonder " was based by Mrs. Centlivre upon the comedy of " The Wrangling Lovers, or The Invisible Mistress," written by Edward Ravenscroft, produced at Dorset Garden, London, in 1676, and printed in 1677. In " The Wrangling Lovers " the scene is Toledo. *Don Diego* and *Octavia* are the lovers, and they continually fluctuate between quarrel and reconciliation. *Elvira* is the name of the Invisible Mistress. The plot of that piece was derived from a story, on a Spanish subject, called " Deceptio Visus, or Seeing and Believing are Two Things "—a work that seems also to have prompted Corneille's " Engagements du Hazard," and Molière's " Dépit Amoureux." Mrs. Centlivre might have borrowed from the Spanish romance or from either

* " I differ from you about the refinement which has banished the comedies of Congreve. Are not the comedies of Sheridan acted to the thinnest houses? I know (as ex-*committed*) that ' The School for Scandal ' was the worst stock-piece upon record. I also know that Congreve gave up writing because Mrs. Centlivre's balderdash drove his comedies off. So it is not decency but stupidity that does all this ; for Sheridan is as decent a writer as Mrs. Centlivre, of whom Wilks, the actor, said, ' not only her play (' The Busybody ') would be damned, but she too.' "—*Lord Byron. Letter to John Murray. Dated Ravenna, March* 29, 1820. Lord Byron, it will be remembered, was one of a committee that managed Drury Lane Theatre in 1815.

of those French plays. The fact that she imitated Ravenscroft appears from similarity of dialogue in the two pieces :

| *From " The Wrangling Lovers."*—1677. | *From " The Wonder."*—1714. |
|---|---|
| *Diego.* All you can do for the future shall be indifferent to me. I will abandon your empire with a facility that shall sufficiently discover that your chains are not so difficult to be broken as your vanity does make you believe. | *Felix.* All you do shall be indifferent to me for the future, and you shall find me abandon your empire with so little difficulty that I'll convince the world your chains are not so hard to break as your vanity would tempt you to believe. |
| *Octavia.* I find you very full of temerity in presuming to say you abandon me— you whom I have so often ordained never to see me more ; but have no sooner banished you my presence but I have seen you at my feet imploring my grace. . . . If my chains, as you scornfully say, are so easy to be broken, why have you not done it twenty times before ? Either they are more powerful than your malice will allow, or you are a very weak man, Don Diego. | *Violante.* This is not to be borne. Insolent ! You abandon ! You ! whom I have so often forbade ever to see me more ! Have you not fallen at my feet ? Implored my favor and forgiveness ? Did you not trembling wait, and wish and sigh and swear yourself into my heart ? Ungrateful man ! If my chains are so easily broken as you pretend, then you are the silliest coxcomb living you did not break 'em long ago ; and I must think him capable of brooking anything, on whom such usage could make no impression. |

This resemblance was remarked by the vigilant eye of Genest, and to him also the reader is indebted for the cast of characters (likewise significant of similarity between the plays) with which the comedy of " The Wrangling Lovers " was produced—a cast that includes several noted names :

| | |
|---|---|
| DON DIEGO ............................ | Smith. |
| DON GUZMAN........ .................... | Harris. |
| SANCO, his Servant...................... | Cave Underhill. |
| COUNT DE BENEVENT, Father to Octavia.... | Leigh. |
| DON RUIS, in love with Octavia............ | Medbourne. |
| ORDGANO, Servant to Don Diego........... | Percival. |
| OCTAVIA..... ...................... | Mrs. Hughes. |
| ELVIRA, Sister to Don Ruis................ | Mrs. Barry. |
| BEATRICE, Woman to Octavia............. | Mrs. Gibbs. |
| JACINTA, Woman to Elvira................. | Mrs. Gillow. |

The record of " The Wonder " on the stage begins with its production, at Drury Lane, April 27, 1714. Success had not been anticipated for it, but its advent was hailed with delight, and the praise of it was soon upon every lip. Rowe's tragedy of " Jane Shore," produced in the same season and by the same company, and heralded with prognostication of ample favor, fell far behind it in popularity. Wilks was the first *Don Felix*, and Mrs. Oldfield the first *Violante*, and Mrs. Centlivre afterward wrote, with reference to their acting in the culminating quarrel scene (Act V.), that " if Nature herself were to paint a love quarrel she could only copy them." *Isabella* was acted by Mrs. Santlowe—the voluptuous beauty who subsequently married Barton Booth. *Flora* was played by Mrs. Saunders, and *Inis* by Mrs. Cox. Mills acted *Colonel Britton ; Lissardo* was represented by Pack, and *Gibby* by Bullock. Wilks, in his time, had no competitor as *Don Felix*, and probably it was in that character, and in kindred parts, that he deserved the significant encomium that was passed upon him by Steele : " To beseech gracefully, to approach respectfully, to pity, to mourn, to love, are the places wherein Wilks may be said to shine with the utmost beauty."

*Don Felix* must have dash and sparkle, must be a master of raillery and sarcasm, must be impetuous and variable—passing swiftly from mood to mood ; but, above all else, he must be a lover, passionately in earnest, and a prey to all the hopes and fears and doubts and longings and worries and caprices that appertain to a lover's condition. That brilliant comedian Lester Wallack, who took that view of the character of *Don Felix*, was especially fine in it, because of his commingled piquancy and ardor. One of the most delightful of his many strokes of feeling was accomplished with the supplication in the quarrel scene ; and no one who heard him say, " Violante, won't you ? " will ever forget it. The rapid change to jealous doubt that followed it was deliciously comical. Wallack was at his best in *Don Felix*, and this age has not seen so good a representative of the part.

Various revivals of " The Wonder "—several of them important because of the distinguished players who were involved—occurred in London before the close of the eighteenth century. On November 14, 1733, at Covent Garden, *Don Felix* and *Violante* were acted by Mr. and Mrs. Giffard, and *Colonel Britton* and *Lissardo* by Delane and Pinkethman. Mrs. Roberts was *Flora*. On November 1, 1734, at the same theatre, Hallam assumed *Don Pedro*, with Mrs. Horton as *Violante.* On January 12, 1774, at Drury Lane, *Don Felix* and *Violante* were acted by Mr. and Mrs. Giffard, with Mrs. Roberts as *Flora*, and Delane as *Colonel Britton.* Yates played *Lissardo.* Mr. and Mrs. Giffard seem to have been long identified with the leading parts in " The Wonder," and Giffard may be accounted the successor to Wilks, who died in 1729. The comedy was acted on April 15, 1748, at Covent Garden, with Mr. and Mrs. Giffard in the chief parts, for the benefit of Mrs. Storer. On March 25, 1756, at Covent Garden, Peg Woffington enacted *Violante* for the first time, and the comic genius of Shuter was expended upon *Gibby*. In the same year, on November 6, at Drury Lane, Garrick first impersonated *Don Felix*, and thenceforward till his retirement from the stage, June 10, 1776—when he chose it for his farewell—he never relinquished the part and he never had an equal in it. Mrs. Macklin was his first *Violante*, while *Flora* was played, very brilliantly we may be sure, by Kitty Clive. *Lissardo* was allotted to Woodward, and *Colonel Britton* to Palmer. Ross was the next *Don Felix*, with Miss Macklin as *Violante*, at Covent Garden, February 17, 1761. Shuter played *Gibby*, Mrs. Pitt was *Flora*, Mrs. Burden *Isabella*, and Mrs. Green *Inis.* At Covent Garden, on November 27, 1767, Powell acted *Don Felix*. Garrick revived " The Wonder," on April 24, 1769, at Drury Lane, on the night of Kitty Clive's last appearance—playing *Don Felix* as only he could play it, with the enchanting Mrs. Barry as *Violante*, and with King as *Lissardo*. Clive presented *Flora*, and there is Tate Wilkinson's testimony that Clive made *Flora* equal to *Violante* and to *Don Felix*. The comedy had yet another fine cast when given, at the same house, on January 20, 1775 : *Don Felix*, Garrick ; *Violante*, Mrs. Yates ; *Colonel Britton*, Jefferson (great-grandfather of the present Joseph Jefferson) ; *Isabella*, Mrs. Jefferson ; *Lissardo*, King ; *Flora*, Mrs. Pope ; *Inis*, Mrs. Bradshaw ; *Gibby*, Johnston ; *Don Lopez*, Baddeley ; *Don Pedro*, Parsons. Later in 1775, on October 20, " The Wonder " was performed at Covent Garden, and Lewis appeared as *Don Felix*, with Mrs. Barry as *Violante*, Quick as *Don Pedro*, and Woodward as *Lissardo*. On December 3, 1784, playing at Covent Garden, Holman assumed *Don Felix*, with Miss Younge as *Violante*, and the irrepressible John Edwin as *Lissardo*. At Drury Lane, on January 3, 1787 (Garrick was now dead, January 20, 1779), Smith assumed *Don Felix*, and the exquisite Miss Farren played *Violante*, while Mrs. Pope was cast for *Flora*, Mrs. Ward for *Isabella*, Woodward for *Lissardo*, and Moody (the Irish pioneer of the drama in America) for *Gibby*. The next notable distribution of the characters in that gay fabric of fun and feeling was made at Drury Lane, January 10, 1797, when John Philip Kemble played *Don Felix* (in which it is difficult to imagine him at ease), with Miss Farren as *Violante*, Miss Pope as *Flora*, Miss Mellon as *Inis*, Miss De Camp (whom Charles Kemble subsequently married) as *Isabella*, Wroughton, now remembered as the old prompter, as *Colonel Britton*, and the younger Bannister as *Lissardo*. George Frederick Cooke presented himself as *Don Felix*, June 7, 1808, at Covent Garden, and most portentous he must have been, with his tragical countenance and his sardonic humor. Miss Smith then played *Violante*, and Mrs. Mattocks—taking a benefit and making her last appearance—played *Flora*. *Colonel Britton* was taken by Brunton, and *Lissardo* by Fawcett. A performance of " The Wonder," on August 5, 1819, at the London Haymarket, presented Mrs. Edwin as *Violante*, Mrs. Gibbs as *Flora*, Mr. Warde as *Don Felix*, Miss E. Blanchard as *Isabella*, Terry as *Gibby*, and Liston as *Lissardo*. Charles Kemble was *Don Felix* when the comedy was revived at Drury Lane, October 22, 1822, with Miss Chester as *Violante*, the superb Miss Foote as *Isabella*, Mrs. Gibbs as *Flora*, and Fawcett as *Lissardo*. Hallam, Elliston, Charles Kean, Macready, Finn, Vandenhoff, Thomas Barry, Hamblin, and Lester Wallack, as *Don Felix*, and Dora Jordan, Mrs. Glover, Ellen Tree, Julia Bennett Barrow, and Mrs. Hoey, as *Donna Violante*, are recorded among the actors of the present century who have illustrated "The Wonder" and gained the public admiration in their fine artistic service. The loveliest *Violante* of that group seems to have been Dora Jordan. Macready, who acted with her in 1812, has left an expressive tribute to her excellence : " With a spirit of fun that would have out-laughed Puck himself, there was a discrimination, an identity with her character, an artistic arrangement of the scene, that made all appear spontaneous and accidental, though elaborated with the greatest care. Her voice was one of the most melodious I ever heard, which she could vary by certain bass tones that would have disturbed the gravity of a hermit. . . . Her laugh was so rich, so apparently irrepressible, so deliciously self-enjoying, as to be at all times irresistible. . . . I have seen many *Violantes* since, but where was there one who could, like her, excite the bursts of rapture in an audience when she recovered from the deadly agony into which her fears of discovery had thrown her, and prepared herself for her triumph over her jealous lover ? The mode in which she taught the *Flora* to act her part was a lesson to make an actress." Surely in that picture there is an instructive lesson in the art of acting.

## II.

Mrs. Centlivre died in 1723. Mrs. Cowley (1743-1809) was born about twenty years later, and Mrs. Cowley's first play was published in 1776. The same quick spirit that was in the one reappeared in the other, but Mrs. Cowley was much the more refined spirit and the more polished writer. The taste, furthermore, had changed with the time. The empire of Dryden had been succeeded by the empire of Dr. Johnson, and Wilks and his compeers had given place to Quin and Garrick. The maiden name of Mrs. Cowley was Parkhouse, and she was born at Tiverton, in Devonshire. Her paternal grandmother was a first cousin to the poet Gay. Her father was a scholar. She was well nurtured and well taught, and her talents as a writer were early and prosperously developed. About 1772 she became the wife of Captain Cowley, of the East India Company's service, and with him she lived in great happiness. Her life was domestic, and she had the wisdom to prize a happy home, the reality of love, and the development of a pure character, beyond literary reputation and the fuss and fever of publicity. She was not a genius, but her talent was genuine and considerable, and the worst that can be said of her as a writer is that she was the "Anna Matilda" of the "Della Crusca" poems—Robert Merry, who married Miss Brunton, being the "Della Crusca." Mrs. Cowley wrote the following plays : "The Runaway," comedy, 1776; "Who's the Dupe?" farce, 1779; "Albina," tragedy, 1779; "The Belle's Stratagem," comedy, 1780; "The School for Eloquence," interlude, 1780; "The World as It Goes," also called "Second Thoughts are Best," comedy, 1781; "Which is the Man?" comedy, 1782; "A Bold Stroke for a Husband," comedy, 1783; "More Ways Than One," comedy, 1784; "The School for Graybeards," comedy, 1786; "The Fate of Sparta," tragedy,* 1788; "A Day in Turkey," comedy, 1792; and "The Town Before You," comedy, 1795. She died at Tiverton, March 11, 1809. Garrick revised her first piece, "The Runaway," and wrote an epilogue for it; and it was the last piece that he received at Drury Lane prior to his withdrawal as actor and manager. There was an epistolary controversy over the tragedy of "Albina," between the author and Miss Hannah More. "The School for Graybeards" was based on Aphra Behn's "Lucky Chance." Several of her pieces failed, but, on the other hand, several of them succeeded beyond the expectations of friends. "The Belle's Stratagem" had the good fortune to please Queen Charlotte, and by her order it was performed before the royal family of George III. once every season for several years.

The stage career of "The Belle's Stratagem" began at Covent Garden, on February 22, 1780. The original *Doricourt* was Lewis—a prince of comedians—and the original *Letitia Hardy* was Miss Younge. Genest records that Edwin's name was in the bill the first two nights, and that the piece was acted twenty-eight times. Twelve years later, the comedy being revived at the same house—February 6, 1792—Fawcett played *Flutter*. On March 22, 1790, at Drury Lane, Dora Jordan taking a benefit, "The Belle's Stratagem" was given, with a remarkable cast: *Doricourt*, J. P. Kemble; *Hardy*, Baddeley; *Sir George Touchwood*, Wroughton; *Flutter*, Bannister, Jr.; *Saville*, Barrymore; *Villers*, Whitfield; *Courtall*, R. Palmer; *Letitia Hardy*, Dora Jordan; *Mrs. Racket*, Miss Pope; *Lady Frances Touchwood*, Mrs. Kemble. On January 8, 1808, at Covent Garden, *Doricourt* was played by Lewis; *Hardy* by Munden—certainly a comic genius of the first order; *Sir George Touchwood* by Murray; *Flutter* by Jones; *Saville* by Brunton; *Letitia Hardy* by Mrs H. Johnston; and *Mrs. Racket* by Mrs. Mattocks. On September 12, 1817, at Covent Garden, Miss Brunton made her first appearance in London, acting *Letitia Hardy*. That was the lady who afterward married Merry, came to America, and after Merry's death became Mrs. Wignell,

---

* The following epigram was made upon it, when it was first acted:

"Ingenious Cowley! while we view'd
Of Sparta's sons the fate severe,
We caught the Spartan fortitude,
And saw their woes without a tear."

and finally Mrs. Warren, step-mother to the veteran Boston comedian (deceased), William Warren. Charles Kemble assumed *Doricourt*. Fawcett played *Hardy*. *Lady Touchwood* was enacted by Miss Foote, and *Mrs. Racket* by Mrs. Gibbs. In a revival of the comedy at Drury Lane on January 20, 1818, *Hardy* was enacted by Dowton, *Flutter* by Harley, *Letitia* by Miss Smithson, of Dublin, and *Mrs. Racket* by the piquant Mrs. Glover. On the American stage it had its first representation January 6, 1794, at the theatre in John Street, New York, with Hodgkinson and his wife as *Doricourt* and *Letitia*, and Hallam as *Flutter*. Murdoch played *Doricourt* at the Old Park, in 1839. On August 30, 1852 "The Belle's Stratagem" was performed at Niblo's, with Charles Wheatleigh as *Doricourt*. It has since been done in many cities of the republic, and with notably good casts.

With the generation of old play-goers, now receding, "The Belle's Stratagem" was a favorite when Wallack's Theatre was in its prime, and also it will be recalled by them as a prominent feature in the repertory of Jean Davenport (Mrs. Lander), when that sterling actress used to present *Letitia Hardy*, with William Wheatley as *Doricourt*. It is almost the only one of Mrs. Cowley's comedies that has practically survived, and Mr. Daly's new version of it, while omitting the most of two acts, preserves its story and its essential elements. It is known that Mrs. Cowley was a charming woman—intellectual, refined, sprightly, and of affectionate disposition and gentle manners ; but that might have been gathered from her writings, even if it had not been recorded. Ideals of character and conduct inevitably indicate the nature from which they spring. The persons in "The Belle's Stratagem" are representative persons, and they manifest exactly what their author considered to be best and most delightful in life. *Letitia Hardy* is an enchanting beauty, luxuriant in health and spirits, unconventional, capable of the fondest love, but also capable, as she herself declares, of being the soul of whim and the spirit of variety, and of resenting ill-treatment by an impetuous and scornful defiance of the proprieties and the world. *Doricourt*, though a man of pleasure, is a man of principle—young, handsome, ardent, gay, and he will take the world lightly, doing no harm in it, but making merriment all around him. If a misfortune falls upon him, he declares, it will sink at once to the bottom of his heart, like a pebble in the water, and leave the surface unruffled. *Mrs. Racket*, the qualified flirt, is the incarnation of good-natured vivacity, and there are few lines in comedy that have a neater point than her remark, to the perplexed cavalier, that if he is really resolved to visit the other world he may as well take one night of pleasure in this. All along the current of the play there are kindred denotements of the healthful and vivacious spirit beneath it. *Flutter*—who is all that his name implies—fails not to please with that self-same quality of buoyant mirth ; and nowhere so fully as in one sentence, spoken by him, has the writer conveyed the characteristic tone of her mind. " Your wise men," exclaims *Flutter*, " are the greatest fools upon earth—for they reason about their enjoyments and analyze their pleasures." It is more than a hundred years since that was said, and the wise men are still reasoning and analyzing, and still the roses bloom. Sprightly and blythe was Mrs. Cowley, and full of joy is her comedy of " The Belle's Stratagem ; " and the audience of to-day heeds no more than did the audience of her own period that the work is neither original nor probable. Congreve and Farquhar were not unremembered in Mrs. Cowley's day, and her style was somewhat modelled after those brilliant originals. " The Belle's Stratagem " is reminiscent of Congreve's " Love for Love " and Farquhar's " Inconstant." The same old situation recurs. The boy and the girl have been betrothed, but the young man and the young woman insist upon the romance of their youth, and there can be no marriage unless there is also love. The lady will act the gawk and thus will change her swain's mood from indifference to aversion, and then, as a stranger, masked and disguised, she will attract and fascinate him. The youth will act the lunatic, in order to escape from his dreaded marriage, and at last will go almost distracted with joy to find himself tricked into a union with the woman whom he loves. That was a favorite theme with the writers of English comedy in the last century. The gentleman often goes mad in jest and the lady often stoops to conquer. In " The Belle's Stratagem " the manner is artificial and the expedients are improbable ; but at least that artificiality is consistently sustained, and you understand that you are looking, not at actual life, but at a delicate exaggeration of it—of which, at the same time, the elements are real. Your logic would readily invalidate the rationality of *Letitia* and *Doricourt :* your senses, all the same, perceive them as delightful and lovable human creatures.

Ada Rehan obtained a triumphant success as *Letitia Hardy.* Her portrayal of *Letitia's* assumed awkwardness was easily perfect. Her adroit use of the Milkmaid song cast a glow of delicious humor, commingled with the perplexing spell of a latent refinement, over that image of rosy rusticity ; and it was quite possible to sympathize with *Doricourt's* bewilderment when he said that he had seen in her eyes an expression that seemed to mock the folly of her lips. The essential attribute of *Letitia Hardy* is feminine fascination—and that was imparted by Ada Rehan to every fibre of the embodiment. In the masquerade scene the victorious air was sustained with inflexible refinement and undeviating grace, and those exquisite speeches about the ideal woman—so easily spoiled and so difficult to deliver—came off in rippling tones of the most musical voice and the most melodious English now heard upon our stage. In demeanor, likewise—in the preservation of a certain stateliness and high-bred isolation—the actress was at her best, and unimpeachable. No one of her predecessors as *Letitia Hardy* (looking back, at least, as far as the springtime of Julia Bennett Barrow) has acted the part with a more intrinsic loftiness of woman-like spirit, with more dignity and grace of bearing, or with a more fortunate assumption of rustic silliness in the hoyden scene ; and no one of them has made it so essentially diffusive of woman-like allurement.* In that particular the characteristic embodiments of Miss Rehan have seldom been equalled. The secret of that allurement is elusive. Among its elements are passionate sincerity, the manifest capability of imparting great happiness, triumphant personal beauty, which yet is touched and softened by a wistful and sympathetic sadness, and that controlling and compelling instinct—essentially feminine—which endows with vital import every experience of love, and creates a perfect illusion in scenes of fancied bliss or woe. The piquant aspect of the character of *Letitia Hardy* was heightened and made the more delightful in Miss Rehan's impersonation because of the emphasis that she laid upon its gravity, making the personality genuine and imparting to *Letitia's* stratagem a momentous importance. In actual life no woman ever really approves of levity and laughter over affairs of the heart. Those are serious things, and throughout all her performances in artificial comedy, whether old or new, Miss Rehan has been felicitous beyond precedent in her fidelity to that instinct of earnest womanhood. The common practice of the stage has been, in all such characters as *Letitia*, to aim only at sparkle and dash. The victorious excellence and artistic superiority of Miss Rehan's assumption were obvious in its union of glittering impetuosity and merry witchery with true passion, womanlike tenderness of heart, and the many sweet ways and innocent wiles with which a loving woman involuntarily commends herself to the object of her love. The embodiment was not a frolic, but a round, coherent, truthful, fascinating portrayal of human nature.

* On the same night Miss Rehan enacted *Mockworld*, in a fanciful and romantic play, by Miss Clo Graves, called "The Knave," and in the two characters she sounded every note in a wide scale of human and poetic emotion.

# THE

# BELLE'S STRATAGEM

CONDENSED FROM Mrs. COWLEY'S COMEDY

*AND ARRANGED IN THREE ACTS*

BY

AUGUSTIN DALY

As First Produced at Daly's Theatre
New York, January 3, 1893

Printed from the Prompt Book of Daly's Theatre

1893

# CHARACTERS.

| CHARACTERS. | Original cast. Covent Garden, February 22, 1780. | Original production in New York,* January 6, 1794. | Cast of Daly's Theatre, January 3, 1893. |
|---|---|---|---|
| DORICOURT.......... | Wm. T. Lewis.... | Hodgkinson....... | Arthur Bourchier. |
| FLUTTER............ | Lee Lewis........ | Hallam.......... | Herbert Gresham. |
| HARDY.............. | Quick............ | Prigmore........ | James Lewis. |
| SAVILLE............ | Aiken............ | ........... | Sidney Herbert. |
| COURTALL.......... | Robson.......... | ........... | John Craig. |
| VILLIERS........... | Whitfield......... | ........... | Wilfred Buckland. |
| FOOTMAN TO DORICOURT... | ........... | ........... | Young. |
| SERVANT TO HARDY...... | ........... | ........... | George Wharnock. |
| **MASQUERADERS.** | | | |
| LETITIA HARDY ...... | Miss Younge..... | Mrs. Hodgkinson.. | Miss Ada Rehan. |
| MRS. RACKETT ...... | Mrs. Matlocks .... | Mrs. Melmoth .... | Adelaide Prince. |
| MISS OGLE.......... | Mrs. Morton...... | ........... | Lotta Lynne. |
| FOLLY ............. | ........... | ........... | Sophia Hoffman. |

* Seilhamer gives the date of June 12. 1786, as that of the original production in New York, but offers no cast.

# THE BELLE'S STRATAGEM.

## ACT I.

### SCENE 1.—*At* DORICOURT'S.

*Enter* COURTALL *and* SAVILLE, R.—*shaking hands as though they had just met.*

*Sav.* Why, and is it you, my dear Courtall! I haven't seen you in an age! You're just going?

*Court.* Yes. Haven't a moment to waste. Just made a call on our returned traveller here. But, pr'ythee, what brings you to town?

*Sav.* I came to meet our friend Doricourt also, who I hear is lately arrived from Rome.

*Court.* Arrived! Yes, faith, and has cut us all out! His carriage, his liveries, himself, are the rage of the day! His first appearance set the whole town in a ferment, and his valet is besieged by levees of tailors, habit makers, and other ministers of fashion, to gratify the impatience of their customers for becoming *à la mode de Doricourt*.

*Sav.* Indeed! Well, those little gallantries will soon be over; he's on the point of marriage.

*Court.* Marriage! Doricourt on the point of marriage! 'Tis the happiest tidings you could have given, next to his being hanged. Who is the bride elect?

*Sav.* I never saw her; but 'tis Miss Hardy, the rich heiress —the match was made by the parents, and the courtship began on their nurses' knees; master used to crow at miss, and miss used to chuckle at master.

19

*Court.* O! then by this time they care no more for each other than I do for my country cousins.

*Sav.* I don't know that; they have never met since thus high, and so, probably, have some regard for each other.

*Court.* Never met! Odd!

*Sav.* A whim of Mr. Hardy's; he thought his daughter's charms would make a more forcible impression, if her lover remained in ignorance of them till his return from the continent.

*Enter* DORICOURT'S FOOTMAN.

*Footman.* M'sieur, my lor' Doricourt will have ze honare to wait upon you immediately. Vill you be seat? [*Exit.*

*Court.* Then I'm off. But promise to dine with me to-day. I have some honest fellows! [*Going.*

*Sav.* Can't promise! Perhaps I may.

*Court.* Ta-ta, then! I'll expect you. [*Exit* L.

*Sav.* I'm glad he couldn't stay. I prefer to meet my old friend alone.

*Enter* DORICOURT, R.

*Doric.* My dear Saville, let the warmth of this embrace speak the pleasure of my heart.

*Sav.* Well, this is some comfort, after the scurvy reception I met with in your hall. I prepared my mind, as I came upstairs, for a *bon jour*, a grimace, and an *adieu.*

*Doric.* Why so?

*Sav.* Judging of the master from the rest of the family. What the deuce is the meaning of that flock of foreigners below, with their parchment faces and snuffy whiskers? What! can't an Englishman stand behind your carriage, buckle your shoe, or brush your coat?

*Doric.* Stale, my dear Saville, stale! Englishmen make the best soldiers, citizens, and philosophers in the world; but the very worst footmen. [*Crosses* L.] I keep French fellows and Germans, as the Romans kept slaves; because their own countrymen had minds too enlarged and haughty to descend with a grace to the duties of such a station.

*Sav.* A good excuse for a bad practice.

*Doric.* On my honor, experience will convince you of its truth.

*Sav.* Never—never. But to start a subject which must please you. When do you expect Miss Hardy in town ?

*Doric.* O, the hour of expectation is past. She is arrived, and I this morning had the honor of an interview at the lawyers. The writings were ready ; and, in obedience to the will of Mr. Hardy, we met to sign and seal.

*Sav.* Has the event answered ? Did your heart leap or sink when you beheld your mistress ?

*Doric.* Faith, neither one nor t'other ; she's a fine girl, as far as mere flesh and blood goes. [*Crosses* R.] But——

*Sav.* But what ?

*Doric.* Why, she's only a fine girl ; complexion, shape, and features ; nothing more.

*Sav.* Is not that enough ?

*Doric.* No ! she should have spirit ! fire ! *l'air enjoué !* that something, that nothing, which everybody feels, and which nobody can describe, in the resistless charmers of Italy and France.

*Sav.* Thanks to the parsimony of my father, that kept me from travel ! I would not have lost my relish for true, unaffected English beauty, to have been quarrelled for by all the belles of Versailles and Florence.

*Doric.* Pho ! thou hast no taste. English beauty ! 'Tis insipidity ; it wants the zest, it wants poignancy, Frank ! Why, I have known a French woman, indebted to nature for no one thing but a pair of decent eyes, reckon in her suite as many counts, marquesses, and *petits maîtres,* as would satisfy three dozen of our first-rate toasts. I have known an Italian marchessina make ten conquests in stepping from her carriage, and carry her slaves from one city to another, whose real, intrinsic beauty would have yielded to half the little grisettes that pace Mall on a Sunday. [*Crosses* L.

*Sav.* And has Miss Hardy nothing of this ?

*Doric.* If she has, she was pleased to keep it to herself. I was in the room half an hour before I could catch the color of her eyes ; and every attempt to draw her into conversation occasioned so cruel an embarrassment that I was reduced to the necessity of exchanging platitudes about the weather with her father.

*Sav.* So Miss Hardy, with only beauty, modesty, and merit, is doomed to the arms of a husband who will despise her.

*Doric.* You are unjust. Though she has not inspired me with violent passion, my honor secures her felicity.

*Sav.* Come, come, Doricourt ; you know very well that when the honor of a husband is *locum tenens* for his heart, his wife must be as indifferent as himself, if she is not unhappy. But come, I detain you—you seem dressed at all points, and of course have an engagement.

*Doric.* To St. James's. [*Crosses* R.] I dine at Hardy's, and accompany them to the masquerade in the evening. But breakfast with me to-morrow, and we'll talk of our old companions—for I swear to you, Saville, the air of the continent has not effaced one youthful prejudice or attachment.

*Sav.* With an exception to the case of ladies and servants.

*Doric.* True ; there I plead guilty.

[*Exeunt* DORICOURT, R., *and* SAVILLE,· L.

---

SCENE 2.—*At* HARDY'S. *A spacious apartment. A spinet at the* L. *A portrait of* MISS HARDY *on an easel on the* R. *Divan* C.

VILLIERS *is discovered at* R., *reading a book, which he throws aside as* FLUTTER *enters, at back, ushered in by a footman.*

*Flut.* Ha, Villiers, have you seen Mrs. Rackett ? Miss Hardy, I find, is out.

*Vil.* I have not seen her yet. I have made a voyage to Lapland since I came in. [*Flinging away the book.*] A lady at her toilet is as difficult to be moved as a Quaker. [*Yawning. Crosses* L., *and sits.*] What events have happened in the world since yesterday ?—have you heard ?

*Flut.* O yes ; I stopped at Tattersall's, as I came by, and there I found—— But, now I think on't, you shan't know a syllable of the matter ; for I have been informed you never believe above one-half of what I say.

*Vil.* My dear fellow, somebody has imposed upon you most egregiously ! Half ! Why, I never believe one-tenth part of what you say ; that is, according to the plain and literal expression ; but, as I understand you, your intelligence is amusing.

*Flut.* That's very hard, now, very hard. I never related a falsity in my life unless I stumbled on it by mistake ; and if it were otherwise, your dull matter-of-fact people are infinitely obliged to those warm imaginations which soar into fiction to amuse you ; for, positively, the common events of this little dirty world are not worth talking about, unless you embellish them ! Ha ! here comes Mrs. Rackett. Adieu to weeds, I see ! All life !

*Enter* MRS. RACKETT, R. U. E. VILLIERS *rises.*

Enter, madam, in all your charms ! Villiers has been abusing your toilet, for keeping you so long ; but I think we are much obliged to it, and so are you.

*Mrs. R.* How so, pray ? Good-morning t'ye both. Here, here's a hand apiece for you.

　　　　　　　　　[*Crosses to* C. *They kiss her hands.*

*Flut.* [R. H.] How so ? Because it has given you so many beauties. 　　　　　　　　　[*Kisses her hand again.*

*Mrs. R.* [C.] Delightful compliment ! What do you think of that, Villiers ?

*Vil.* [L. H.] That he and his compliments are alike—showy, but won't bear examining. So you brought Miss Hardy to town last night ?

*Mrs. R.* Yes ; I should have brought her before, but I had a fall from my horse, that confined me a week. I suppose, in her heart, she wished me hanged a dozen times an hour.

*Flut.* Why ?

*Mrs. R.* Had she not an expecting lover in town all the

23

time? She meets him this morning at the lawyer's. I hope she'll charm him; she's the sweetest girl in the world.

[*Crosses* R.

*Vil.* Vanity, like murder, will out. You have convinced me you think yourself more charming.

*Mrs. R.* How can that be?

*Vil.* [*Crosses* C.] No woman ever praises another, unless she thinks herself superior in the very perfections she allows.

*Flut.* [L. C.] No man ever rails at the sex, unless he is conscious he deserves their hatred.

*Mrs. R.* Thank ye, Flutter — I'll owe ye a bouquet for that.

*Flut.* Well, don't forget to pay it me when we meet. But good-morning to ye both. I must be off. [*Going up.*] I'm going to Mrs. Crotchett's to hear the last bit of gossip she knows, and tell her the last tit-bit I've heard.

*Vil.* [L.] I'll venture every figure in your tailor's bill you make some blunder there.

*Flut.* [*Turning back—down* R.] Done! my tailor's bill has not been paid these two years; and I'll open my mouth with as much care as Mrs. Bridget Button, who wears cork plumpers in each cheek, and never hazards more than six words, for fear of showing them. [*Exit* L. H. I E.

*Mrs. R.* [*Going up* C.] 'Tis a good-natured, insignificant creature, let in everywhere, and cared for nowhere. [LETITIA *is heard outside.*] There's Miss Hardy, returned from Lincoln's Inn!

*Vil.* Then I leave you. [*Meets* LETITIA, L. U. E.

*Enter* LETITIA, C. *and* L.

I am rejoiced to see you so well, madam! but I must tear myself away. [*Exit* L. U. E.

*Let.* [*Throwing herself on a chair,* C., *and looking in a pocket-glass;* MRS. RACKETT *on* R. H., *staring at her.*] Did you ever see such a fright as I am to-day?

*Mrs. R.* [R.] Yes, I have seen you look much worse.

*Let.* How can you be so provoking? If I do not look this

morning worse than ever I looked in my life I am naturally a fright. You shall have it which way you will.

*Mrs. R.* Just as you please ; but pray what is the meaning of all this ?

*Let.* [*Rising.*] Men are all dissemblers, flatterers, deceivers ! Have I not heard, a thousand times, of my air, my eyes, my shape—all made for victory ? and to-day, when I bent my whole heart on one poor conquest, I have proved that all those imputed charms amount to nothing ; for Doricourt saw them unmoved. [*Crosses* R.] A husband of fifteen months could not have examined me with more cutting indifference.

*Mrs. R.* Then you return it like a wife of fifteen months, and be as indifferent as he.

*Let.* Ay, there's the sting! The happy boy, that left his image in my young heart, is, at eight-and-twenty, improved in every grace that fixed him there. It is the same face that my memory and my dreams constantly painted to me ; but its graces are finished, and every beauty heightened. How mortifying to feel myself at the same moment his slave and an object of perfect indifference to him ! [*Crosses to* L.

*Mrs. R.* How are you certain that was the case ? Did you expect him to kneel down before the lawyer, his clerks, and your father, to make oath of your beauty ?

*Let.* No ; but he should have looked as if a sudden ray had pierced him ; he should have been breathless ! speechless ! for O ! Caroline, all this was I !

*Mrs. R.* I am sorry you were such a fool. Can you expect a man who has courted and been courted by half the fine women in Europe, to feel like a girl from a boarding-school ? [*Crosses* L.] He is the prettiest fellow you have seen, and of course bewilders your imagination ; but he has seen a million of pretty women, child, before he saw you ; and his first feelings have been over long ago.

*Let.* Your raillery distresses me ; but I *will* touch his heart, or never be his wife.

*Mrs. R.* Absurd and romantic ! If you have no reason to believe his heart pre-engaged, be satisfied ; if he is a man of honor, you'll have nothing to complain of.

*Let.* Nothing to complain of? Heavens! shall I marry the man I adore with such an expectation as that?

*Mrs. R.* And when you have fretted yourself pale, my dear, you'll have mended your expectation greatly.

*Let.* [*Pausing.*] Yet I have one hope. If there is any power whose peculiar care is faithful love, that power I invoke to aid me.  [*Crosses* L., *sits.*

*Enter* MR. HARDY, L. U. E.

*Har.* [*Crosses to* C.] Well, now, wasn't I right? Ay, Letty! Ay, Cousin Rackett! wasn't I right? I knew 'twould be so. He was all agog to see her before he went abroad; and if he had 'a seen her, he'd have thought no more of her face, may be, than his own.

*Mrs. R.* [L. H.] May be not half so much.

*Har.* [C.] Ay, may be so; but I foresee things; exactly as I foresaw, to-day he fell desperately in love with the wench —he, he, he!  [*Sits.*

*Let.* [L. H.] Indeed, sir! how did you perceive it?

*Har.* That's a pretty question! How do I perceive everything? How did I foresee the fall of corn, and the rise of taxes? How did I foretell that a war would sink the funds? How did I foresee last Sunday, when a boiled leg of pork came upon the table, that a dish of greens would follow? [LETITIA *falls into chair.*] How did I—but what the devil makes you so dull, Letitia? I thought to have found you popping about, as brisk as the jacks of your harpsichord.

*Let.* Surely, sir, 'tis a very serious occasion.

*Har.* [*Rises.*] Pho! pho! girls should never be grave before marriage. How did you feel, cousin, beforehand, eh?

*Mrs. R.* Feel! why, exceedingly full of cares.

*Har.* Did you, now?

*Mrs. R.* I could not sleep for thinking of my coach, my liveries, and my chairmen; the taste of clothes I should be presented in distracted me for a week; and whether I should be married in white or lilac gave me the most cruel anxiety.

*Let.* [*Rises.*] And is it possible that you felt no other care?

*Har.* And pray, of what sort may your cares be, Mrs. Letitia? I begin to foresee, now, that you have taken a dislike to Doricourt.

*Let.* Indeed, sir, I have not.

*Har.* Then what's all this melancholy about? Ain't you agoing to be married?—and what's more, to a sensible man?—and what's more to a young girl, to a handsome man? And what's all this melancholy for, I say?

*Mrs. R.* Why, because he is handsome and sensible, and because she's over head and ears in love with him; all which, it seems, your foreknowledge had not told you a word of.

*Let.* Fie, Caroline!

*Har.* Well, come, do you tell me what's the matter, then. If you don't like him, hang the signing and sealing—he shan't have you; and yet I can't say that, neither; for you know that estate, that cost his father and me upward of fourscore thousand pounds, must go all to him if you won't have him: if he won't have you, indeed, 'twill be all yours. All that's clear —engrossed upon parchment, and the poor dear man set his hand to it whilst he was a-dying. "Ah," said I, " I foresee you'll never live to see them come together; but their first son shall be christened Jeremiah, whether it's a boy or a girl, after you—that I promise you." But come, I say, what is the matter? Don't you like him?

*Let.* I fear, sir—if I must speak—I fear I was less agreeable in Mr. Doricourt's eyes than he appeared in mine.

*Har.* There you are mistaken; for I asked him, and he told me he liked you vastly. Don't you think he must have taken a fancy to her? *[To* Mrs. RACKETT.

*Mrs. R.* Why, really, I think so, as I was not by.

*Let.* My dear sir, I am convinced he has not; but if there is spirit or invention in woman, he shall.

*Har.* Right. girl; go to your toilet——

[*Embraces* LETITIA, *who goes* C.

*Let.* It is not my toilet that can serve me; but a plan has struck me, if you will not oppose it, which flatters me with brilliant success.

*Har.* Oppose it! Not I, indeed. What is it?

*Let.* Why, sir, it may seem a little paradoxical; but as he does not like me enough, I want him to like me still less, and will at our next interview endeavor to heighten his indifference into dislike.

*Har.* Who the devil could have foreseen that?

*Mrs. R.* [*Crosses to* C.] Letitia, are you serious?

*Let.* As serious as the most important business of my life demands.

*Mrs. R.* [C.] Why endeavor to make him dislike you?

*Let.* Because 'tis much easier to convert a sentiment into its opposite, than to transform indifference into tender passion.

*Mrs. R.* That may be good philosophy, but I'm afraid you'll find it a bad maxim.

*Let.* I have the strongest confidence in it. I am inspired with unusual spirits, and on this hazard willingly stake my chance for happiness. I am impatient to begin my measures.
[*Goes up and down* L.

*Har.* [L. H.] Can you foresee the end of this, Cousin Rackett?

*Mrs. R.* [R. H.] No, sir; nothing less than your penetration can do that, I am sure.

*Har.* Well, 'tis an odd thing; I can't understand it; but I foresee Letty will have her way, so I shan't give myself the trouble to dispute it.

*Enter* SERVANT.

*Ser.* Mr. Doricourt, sir, is below, and wishes to see either Miss Hardy or yourself.

*Har.* I'll go to him. [*Exit* SERVANT, L.] Now—now Letty [*Goes up* L.], think again on what you're doing, or I foresee there will be the devil to pay. [*Exit.*

*Mrs. R.* Come, prepare, prepare—your lover is coming.

*Let.* My lover! If I comprehend him, awkwardness and bashfulness are the last falls he can pardon in a woman; so expect to see me transformed into the veriest maukin.
[*Crosses* R.

*Mrs. R.* [*Goes to her.*] You persevere then?

*Let.* Certainly. I know the design is a rash one, and the

event important ; it either makes Doricourt mine by all the tenderest ties of passion, or deprives me of him forever ; and never to be his wife will afflict me less than to be his wife and not be beloved.

*Mrs. R.* So you won't trust to the good old maxim, " Marry first, and love will follow " ?

*Let.* As readily as I would venture my last guinea that good fortune might follow. The woman that has not touched the heart of a man before he leads her to the altar, has scarcely a chance to charm it when possession and security turn their powerful arms against her.

*Doric.* [*Without* L. H.] Upstairs, hey ?

*Let.* But here he comes. [*Goes up* R.] I'll disappear for a moment. Don't spare me. [*Exit* R. H.

*Enter* DORICOURT, L. H. I E., *not seeing* MRS. RACKETT, *who sits* R.

*Doric.* So ! [*Puts his hat on table. Looking at the picture.*] This is my mistress, I presume. *Ma foi !* the painter has hit her off. The downcast eye—the blushing cheek—timid— apprehensive—bashful. A tear and a prayer-book would have made her La Bella Magdalena——

Give me a woman in whose touching mien
A mind, a soul, a polished art is seen ;
Whose motion speaks, whose poignant air can move ;
Such are the darts to wound with endless love.
[*Backing* C.

*Mrs. R.* [*Rises.*] Bravo ! Bravo ! Is that an impromptu ?

*Doric.* [*Starting.*] Madam ! [*Aside.*] Finely caught ! Not absolutely—it struck me, during the dessert, as a motto for your picture.

*Mrs. R.* Gallantly turned ! I perceive, however, Miss Hardy's charms have made no violent impression on you. And who can wonder ? the poor girl's defects are so obvious.

*Doric.* Defects !

*Mrs. R.* Merely those of education. Her father's indulgence ruined her. *Mauvaise honte*, conceit and ignorance all unite in the lady you are to marry.                    [*Crosses* L.

*Doric.* Marry! I marry such a woman! Your picture, I hope, is overcharged. I marry *mauvaise honte*—pertness and ignorance!

*Mrs. R.* Thank your stars that ugliness and ill-temper are not added to the list. You must think her handsome?

*Doric.* Half her personal beauty would content me; but could the Medicean Venus be animated for me, and endowed with a vulgar soul, I should become the statue, and my heart transformed to marble.

*Mrs. R.* Bless us! We are in a hopeful way, then!

*Doric.* There must be some envy in this. [*Aside.*] I see she is a coquette. Ha, ha, ha! and you imagine I am persuaded of the truth of your character! ha, ha, ha! Miss Hardy, I have been assured, madam, is elegant and accomplished—but one must allow for a lady's painting.

[*Crosses* L. *Bows.*

*Mrs. R.* [*Aside.*] I'll be even with him for that—Ha, ha, ha! and so you have found me out? Well, I protest I meant no harm; 'twas only to increase the *éclat* of her appearance that I threw a veil over her charms.

[LETITIA *is heard outside.*

*Let.* There! Take that! How dare you! [*Noise of slap.*] You crosspatch!

*Mrs. R.* Here comes the lady; her elegance and accomplishments will announce themselves.


*Enter* LETITIA, *running with apple*, I E. R. H.


*Let.* La, cousin, do you know that our John—— O dear heart! I didn't see you, sir.

[*Hanging down her head, and dropping behind* MRS. RACKETT. *Looks at* DORICOURT *through* MRS. RACKETT'S *arm.*

*Mrs. R.* Fie, Letitia—Mr. Doricourt thinks you a woman of elegant manners. Stand forward and confirm his opinion.

*Let.* No, no ; keep before me. He's my sweetheart, and 'tis impudent to look one's sweetheart in the face, you know. He, he, he !                                        [*Idiotic giggle.*

*Mrs. R.* You'll allow in future for a lady's painting, sir—ha, ha, ha !

*Doric.* I am astonished.

*Let.* Well, hang it, I will take heart. Why, he is but a man, you know, cousin—and I'll let him see I wasn't born in a wood to be scared by an owl. [*Crosses* C. *Half apart; advances, and looks at him through her fingers.*] He, he, he ! You have been a great traveller, sir, I hear. They told me you've been all over Greece. I wish you'd tell us about the fine sights you saw when you went over sea. I have read in a book that there are some other countries, where the men and women are all horses. Did you see any of them ? He, he, he !

*Mrs. R.* [R. H.] Mr. Doricourt is not prepared, my dear, for these inquiries—he is reflecting on the importance of the question, and will answer you—when he can.

*Let.* [C.] When he can ! Why, he's as slow in speech as Aunt Margery when she's reading Thomas Aquinas—and stands gaping like mumchance. [*Gets beside* MRS. RACKETT.

*Mrs. R.* Have a little discretion. [*Coming close to* LETITIA.

*Let.* [*snappishly.*] Hold your tongue !—Sure I may say what I please before I am married, if I can't afterward. D'ye think a body does not know how to talk to a sweetheart ? He is not the first I have had !

*Doric.* [L. H.] Indeed !                                   [*Suddenly.*

*Let.* O, lud, it speaks ! Why, if you must know, there was the curate at home. When dad was a-hunting, he used to come a-suitoring, and make speeches to me out of books. Nobody knows what a mort of fine things he used to say to me—and call me Venis, and Jubah, and Dinah, and Cupid, and another little boy.

*Doric.* And pray, fair lady, how did you answer him ?

*Let.* Why, I used to say—[*With arms akimbo.*] "Look you, Mr. Curate, don't think to come over me with your flimflams, for a better man than ever trod in your shoes is coming over sea to marry me." But 'ifags, I begin to think I was out. Parson Dobbins was the sprightfuler man of the two.

[*To* MRS. RACKETT.

*Doric.* Surely this cannot be Miss Hardy?

*Let.* Laws, why, don't you know me? You saw me to-day —but I was daunted before dad and the lawyer, and all them, and did not care to speak out—so maybe you thought I couldn't. But I can talk as fast as anybody when I knows folks a little. [*Goes up stage, skipping, and munching an apple.*

*Enter* HARDY, L., *and gets* R. C.

*Har.* [C.] I foresee this won't do. Mr. Doricourt, maybe you take my daughter for a fool, but you are mistaken; she's as sensible a girl as any in England.

*Doric.* [L. H.] I am convinced she has a very uncommon understanding, sir. [*Aside.*] I did not think he had been such an ass!

*Let.* [R. C., *aside.*] My father will undo the whole. [*Aloud, crossing to him.*] Laws, papa, how can you think he can take me for a fool, when everybody knows I beat the 'pothecary at conundrums last Christmas-time! And didn't I make a string of names, all in riddles, for the Lady's Dairy? [*Gets* L. C., *with her back to* DORICOURT.] There was a little river and a great house: that was Newcastle. There was what a lamb says, and three letters: that was ba, and k-e-r, ker, baker. There was—— [*Turns, leering at* DORICOURT.

*Har.* [*Turns* LETITIA, R.C.] Don't stand ba-a-ing there— you'll make me mad in a moment. I tell you, sir, that for all that, she's devilish sensible.

*Doric.* Sir, I give all possible credit to your assertions.

*Let.* Laws, papa, do go along. [*Crosses to* HARDY, R. C.] If you stand watching, how can my sweetheart break his mind, and tell me how he admires me? [*Down* L.

*Doric.* That would be difficult, indeed, madam.

*Let.* He, he, he!

*Har.* I tell you, Letty, I'll have no more of this. I foresee well enough—— [*Runs her up stage.*

32

*Let.* Laws, don't snub me before my husband—that is to be. You'll teach him to snub me, too—and I believe by his looks he'd like to begin now. So let us go. [HARDY *pulls her to* R. H.] Cousin, you may tell the gentleman what a genus I have—[HARDY *pulls her again.*]—how I can cut watch-papers, and work catgut—[HARDY *pulls her again.*]—make quadrille baskets with pins, and take profiles in shade——[*Pushes* HARDY *off,* I E. R. H.; *running after him, then returns.*] And I can sing, too ! You never heard me sing, did you ? Some people say they never want to hear me again, when I begin. Here, just hold my apple—[*Puts the apple into his hand. He places it on the table.*]—and stand there, and just you judge for yourself. If you get skeer'd just cry out, and I'll run off.

[*Sings.*

Where are you going to, my pretty maid,
Where are you going to, my pretty maid ?
 I'm going a milking, sir, she said ;
 I'm going a milking, sir, she said.


Shall I go with you, my pretty maid,
Shall I go with you, my pretty maid?
 And heartily welcome, sir, she said ;
 And heartily welcome, sir, she said.


Will you marry me, my pretty maid,
Will you marry me, my pretty maid?
 Yes, if you please, kind sir, she said,
 Yes, if you please, kind sir, she said.

[HARDY *puts his head in. Is motioned off by* MRS. RACKETT


And what is your fortune, my pretty maid,
And what is your fortune, my pretty maid?
      [DORICOURT *turns to her.*
 My face is my fortune, sir, she said,
 My face is my fortune, sir, she said.

Then I can't wed you, my pretty maid,
Then I'll not wed you, my pretty maid.
Nobody axed you, sir, she said,
Nobody axed you, sir, she said.

[*At end* HARDY *comes on and drags her off. She struggles to get away, saying:*] Oh, let me sing the rest of it. There are seventeen more verses. [*As she goes off,* DORICOURT *walks up the stage, and down to the table, to pick up his hat;* LETITIA *runs on, picks up her apple, and runs off, saying:*] Ah! I ain't a-going to let you keep my apple.

*Mrs. R.* What think you of my painting now?

*Doric.* O, mere water-colors, madam. The lady has caricatured your picture.

*Mrs. R.* And how does she strike you as a whole?

*Doric.* Like a good design spoiled by the incapacity of the artist. Her faults are evidently the result of her father's weak indulgence. I observed an expression in her eye that seemed to satirize the folly of her lips.

*Mrs. R.* But at her age, when education is fixed, and manner becomes nature, hopes of improvement——

*Doric.* Would be absurd. Besides, I can't turn schoolmaster. Doricourt's wife must be incapable of improvement— but it must be because she's got beyond it.          [*Crosses* R.

*Mrs. R.* I am pleased your misfortune sits no heavier.

*Doric.* Your pardon, madam. So mercurial was the hour in which I was born, that misfortunes always go plump to the bottom of my heart, like a pebble in water, and leave the surface unruffled. I shall certainly set off for Bath, or the other world, to-night—but whether I shall use a chaise with four swift coursers, or go off in a tangent from the aperture of a pistol, deserves consideration—so I make my adieus.

[*Going up* L.

*Mrs. R.* O, but I entreat you, postpone your journey till to-morrow. Determine on which you will, you must be this night at the masquerade.

*Doric.* Masquerade!

*Mrs. R.* Why not? If you resolve to visit the other world, you may as well take one night's pleasure first in this, you know.

*Doric.* Faith, that's very true ; ladies are the best philosophers after all. Expect me at the masquerade. [*Exit* C. L.

*Enter* HARDY, R. H. I E.

*Har.* What, 's he gone ? [*Crosses, up* L.

*Mrs. R.* Yes, and I am glad he is. You would have ruined us ! Now I beg, Mr. Hardy, you won't interfere in this business ; it is a little out of your way. [*Exit* R. H. I E.

*Har.* Hang me if I don't though—I foresee very clearly what will be the end of it if I leave you to yourselves ; so I'll e'en follow him to the masquerade, and tell him all about it. Let me see—what shall my dress be ?—a great mogul ? No. A grenadier ? No—no—that, I foresee, would make a laugh. Hang me if I don't send to the theatre, to that dog little Lewis, and borrow his *Shylock* dress--I know the dog likes a glass of good wine ; so I'll give him a bottle of my forty-eight, and he shall teach me how to play the part. [*Exit* R. H. I E.

CURTAIN.

# ACT II.

*A Masquerade. The curtain rises upon a lively rally and the end of a dance, with* FOLLY *as the central figure.*

HARDY *enters through the crowd dressed as* SHYLOCK *—meeting* VILLIERS, *who is masked. All lift their masks as he talks to them, and replace them as they talk to him.*

*Har.* Why, isn't it a shame to see so many stout, well-built young fellows masquerading and cutting Courantas here at home, instead of making the French cut capers to the tone of cannon, or sweating the Spaniards with an English fandango? I foresee the end of all this.

*Vil.* [*Masked, advances* R. H.] What, my little Shy—— How the devil came you here? Where's your old Margaret?

*Har.* O, I have got rid of her.

*Vil.* How?

*Har.* Why, I persuaded a young Irishman that she was a blooming beauty of eighteen; so they made an elopement— [*Enter* FOLLY, *who dances round* HARDY.]—ha, ha, ha! and she is now the toast of Tipperary.

*Har.* [*To* FOLLY.] Hey! Tomfool! what business have you here?

*Folly.* What, sir! affront a prince in his own dominion?

[*Music.* FOLLY *struts off*, 2 E. R. H.

*Har.* [*Aside, looking off*, 2 E. R. H.] Ha! there's Cousin Rackett and her party; they shan't know me.

[*Puts on his mask. Music.*

36

*Enter* MRS. RACKETT, *in domino,* MISS OGLE, *in domino,*
SAVILLE, *dressed as a conjuror,* COURTALL, *as the
grand mogul, and* FLUTTER, R. H. I E.

*Mrs. R.* Look at this dumpling Jew! You have surely practised the flesh-hook a long time, friend, to have raised that
goodly presence.

*Har.* About as long, my brisk widow, as you have been
angling for a second husband; but my hook has been better
baited than yours. You have only caught gudgeons, I see.
[*Pointing to* FLUTTER.

*Flut.* [*Crosses* R. C.] O, this is one of the Tomfools they
hire to entertain the company with their accidental sallies. Let
me look at your common-place book, friend; I want a few
good things. [*Crosses to* HARDY.

*Har.* I'd oblige you, with all my heart; but you'll spoil them
in repeating—[FLUTTER *goes up and down* L.]—or, if you
should not, they'll gain you no reputation—for nobody will
believe they are your own. [*Crosses* L.

*Miss O.* He knows ye, Flutter! The little gentleman fancies
himself a wit, I see. [*Up and down* R. FLUTTER *turns up.*

*Har.* [*Aside.*] I can neither see Doricourt nor Letty. I must
find them out. [*Exit* HARDY, L. H. U. E.

*Court.* [*Crosses* C.] Well, Mrs. Rackett, is not all this charming?

*Mrs. R.* [L.] Delightful! Enchanting!

*Court.* And yet in a few hours—in a few hours vapidity and
languor will take the place of that exquisite sense of enjoyment which flutters your ladyship's heart.

*Mrs. R.* What an inhuman creature. The Fates have not
allowed us these sensations above ten times in our lives—and
would you have us shorten them by anticipations of next
week's ennui or to-morrow morning's headache?

*Flut.* [*Crosses* C.] O Lord! your wise men are the greatest
fools upon earth, they reason about their enjoyments, and
analyze their pleasures, while the essence escapes. [*Crosses
L. and* C.] Look! D'ye see that figure strutting in the dress
of an emperor? His father retails oranges in Petticoat Lane.
That gypsy is a maid of honor, and that ragman a physician.

*Miss O.* [*Crosses* C.] Why, you know everybody!

*Flut.* O, every creature. A mask is nothing at all to me. I can give you the history of half the people here. In the next apartment there is a whole family, who, to my knowledge, have lived on water-cresses this month to make a figure here to-night; [*All laugh.*] but, to make up for that, they'll cram their pockets with cold ducks and chickens, for ·a carnival to-morrow. [*All laugh.*

*Mrs. R.* O, I should like to see this provident family.

*Flut.* Honor me with your arm.

[*Exeunt* FLUTTER *and* MRS. RACKETT, L. U. E.; COURT-ALL *and* MISS OGLE, R. U. E.

DORICOURT *enters with* SAVILLE, L. U. E.; LETITIA *enters*, R. I E., *through the maze, as if looking for someone.*

*Doric.* [*Looking off. To* SAVILLE.] There's a fine figure. I'll address her. [*Enters Rally No.* I.] Charity, fair lady, charity!—Charity for a poor pilgrim.

*Let.* Charity! If you mean my prayers, Heaven grant thee wit, pilgrim. [*Aside.*] Does he know me—Heaven forbid!

*Doric.* That blessing would do from a devotee; from you I ask other charities; such charities as beauty should bestow—soft looks, sweet words, and kind wishes.

*Let.* Alas! I am bankrupt of these, and forced to turn beggar myself. [*Crosses* R.

*Doric.* Will you grant me no favor?

*Let.* Yes, one—I'll make you my partner—not for life, but through the soft mazes of a gavotte. Dare you dance?

*Sav.* Some spirit in that.

*Doric.* I dare do anything you command. [*Aside to* SAVILLE.] Do you know her?

*Sav.* No. Such a woman as that would formerly have been known in any disguise; but beauty is now common—Venus seems to have given her cestus to the whole sex. [*Crosses* R.

[*Music. A Gavotte, danced by* LETITIA *and* DORICOURT, MRS. RACKETT *and* FLUTTER, MISS OGLE *and* SAVILLE, *and* COURTALL *and a lady. At end of dance,* LETITIA *goes off with a mask.*

*Doric.* She dances divinely. Who can she be? Somebody must know her. [*To* SAVILLE, *who is going off.*] Ha! Saville! Do you know the lady I danced with just now?

*Sav.* No. But where is Miss Hardy? [*Crosses* L.

*Doric.* Cutting watch-papers and making conundrums, I suppose.

*Sav.* What do you mean?

*Doric.* Faith, I hardly know. She's not here, however, Mrs. Rackett tells me. I asked no further.

*Sav.* Your indifference seems increased.

*Doric.* [L. C.] Quite the reverse; 'tis advanced thirty-two degrees toward hatred.

*Sav.* You are jesting!

*Doric.* Then it must be with a very ill grace, my dear Saville; for I never felt so seriously. Do you know the creature's almost an idiot?

*Sav.* What!

*Doric.* An idiot. What the devil shall I do with her? Egad! I think I'll feign myself mad—and then Hardy will propose to cancel the engagement.

*Sav.* [*Crosses* L.] An excellent expedient. I must leave you; you are mysterious, and I can't stay to unravel ye.

[*Business with* LETITIA; *then exit* SAVILLE, R. H. U. E.

*Doric.* [*Musing.*] Yes, I think that will do. I'll feign myself mad, fee the doctor to pronounce me incurable, and when the parchments are destroyed——

[*Stands in a musing posture,* L. C.

*Music. Dance at back. Enter* LETITIA, R. H. 2 E.

*Let.* You have chosen an odd situation for study. Fashion and taste preside in this spot;—they throw their spells around you;—ten thousand delights spring up at their command;—and you, a stoic—a being without senses, are wrapt in reflection.

*Doric.* And you, the most charming being in the world, awaken me to admiration. Did you come from the stars?

*Let.* Yes, and I shall reascend in a moment. [*Crosses* L.

*Doric.* Pray show me your face before you go.

*Let.* Beware of imprudent curiosity ; it lost Paradise.

*Doric.* Eve's curiosity was raised by the devil—'tis an angel tempts mine. So your illusion is not in point.

*Let.* But why would you see my face ?          [*Crosses* R.

*Doric.* To fall in love with it.

*Let.* And what then ?

*Doric.* Why then—— [*Aside.*] Ay, curse it ! there's the rub !

*Let.* Your mistress will be angry; but perhaps you have no mistress ?

*Doric.* Yes, yes, and a sweet one it is !

*Let.* What ! is she old?

*Doric.* No.

*Let.* Ugly ?

*Doric.* No.

*Let.* What then ?

*Doric.* Pho ! don't talk about her ; but show me your face.

*Let.* My vanity forbids it—'twould frighten you.

*Doric.* Impossible ! Your shape is graceful, your air bewitching, and your chin would tempt me to kiss it, if I did not see a pouting red lip above it, that demands——

[*Going to kiss.*

*Let.* You grow too free.          [*Crosses to* L. H.

*Doric.* Show me your face, then—only half a glance.

*Let.* Not for worlds !

[*A short rally here,* FOLLY *leading the way ; or a short Bacchanalian chorus.* DORICOURT *and* LETITIA, *lost for a moment in the maze, come together again at the end.*

*Doric.* [R.] By heaven, I never was charmed till now. English beauty ! French vivacity—wit—elegance ! [*To* LE-TITIA.] Your name, my angel—tell me your name, though you persist in concealing your face.

*Let.* [L.] My name has a spell in it.

*Doric.* I thought so ; it must be charming.

*Let.* But if revealed, the charm is broke.

*Doric.* I'll answer for its force.

*Let.* [*Crosses* R.] Suppose it Harriet, or Charlotte, or Maria, or——

*Doric.* Hang Harriet, and Charlotte, and Maria!—the name your father gave ye?

*Let.* That can't be worth knowing, 'tis so transient a thing.

*Doric.* How transient?

*Let.* Heaven forbid my name should be lasting till I am married.                                        •

*Doric.* Married! the chains of matrimony are too heavy and vulgar for such a spirit as yours. The flowery wreaths of Cupid are the only bands you should wear.

*Let.* They are the lightest, I believe; but 'tis possible to wear those of marriage gracefully. Throw them loosely round, and twist them in a true lover's knot for the bosom.

[*Crosses* L.

*Doric.* An angel! But what will you be when a wife!

*Let.* A woman. If my husband should prove a churl, a fool, or a tyrant, I'd break his heart, ruin his fortune, elope with the first pretty fellow that asked me, and return the contempt of the world with scorn, while my feelings preyed upon my life.                     [*Crosses up stage, then down* R.

*Doric.* [L.] Amazing! [*Aside.*] What if you loved him, and he were worthy of your love?

*Let.* Why, then I'd be anything and all!—grave, gay, capricious—the soul of whim, the spirit of variety—live with him in the eye of fashion, or in the shade of retirement—change my country, my sex—feast with him in an Esquimaux hut, or a Persian pavilion—join him in the victorious war-dance on the borders of Lake Ontario, or sleep to the soft breathings of the flute in the cinnamon groves of Ceylon—dig with him in the mines of Golconda, or enter the dangerous precincts of the mogul's seraglio—cheat him of his wishes, and overturn his empire, to restore the husband of my heart to the blessings of liberty and love.                                        [*Up* R.

*Doric.* Delightful wildness! O, to catch thee, and hold thee forever in this little cage!     [*Attempting to clasp her.*

*Let.* Hold, sir. Though Cupid must give the bait that tempts me to the snare, 'tis Hymen must spread the net to catch me.

*Doric.* 'Tis in vain to assume airs of coldness ; fate has or-dained you mine.

*Let.* How do you know ?

*Doric.* I feel it here. I never met with a woman so per-fectly to my taste ; and I won't believe it formed you so, on purpose to tantalize me.

*Let.* [*Aside.*] This moment is worth a whole existence.

*Doric.* Come, show me your face, and rivet my chains.

*Let.* To-morrow you shall be satisfied.

*Doric.* To-morrow, and not to-night ?

*Let.* No.

*Doric.* Where, then, shall I wait on you to-morrow ?—where see you ?

*Let.* You shall see me at an hour when you least expect me.

*Doric.* Why all this mystery ?

*Let.* I like to be mysterious. At present be content to know that I am a woman of family and fortune.

*Doric.* Let me see you to your carriage.

*Let.* As you value knowing me, stir not a step. [*Dodges under his arm, as he makes a dash to clasp her.*] If I am fol-lowed, you never see me more. [LETITIA *runs off* R. I E., *followed by* DORICOURT. HARDY *toddles on after them.* LETITIA *reappears*, R. U. E., *and escapes among a group of maskers who come on after* HARDY. DORICOURT *runs on and is whirled about among them, and* HARDY *runs after, puffing and blowing.*] Adieu. *Exit* R. H. I E.

[*Second Rally.*]

*Doric.* Barbarous creature ! she's gone ! What ! Am I in love ? Pho ! it can't be.


*Enter* FLUTTER *and* HARDY, R. H. 2 E.

O, Flutter, do you know that charming creature ?

*Flut.* What charming creature ? I passed a thousand.

*Doric.* [R. C.] She went out at that door, as you entered.

*Flut.* [C.] O, yes ; I know her very well.

*Doric.* Do you, my dear fellow ? Who——

*Flut.* Why, she's the most terrible coquette and enchantress in town. She's jilted and been jilted by half a hundred men about town.

*Har.* [*Up.*] Impudent scoundrel! I foresee I'll cut his throat.

*Doric.* Jilt and coquette!

*Flut.* Yes! First she had Lord George Jennett on a string, then Colonel Gorget, next old man Lovell had spasms about her, then I came in for a turn; and I don't know who else. But Lord George Jennett is at her feet again.

· [*Goes up and talks to other masks, and goes off* U. E. R.

*Doric.* I'll murder Gorget, poison Lord George, and shoot myself. [*Crosses* L.

*Har.* Now's the time, I see, to clear up the whole. Mr. Doricourt! I say, Flutter was mistaken: I know who you are in love with. [*Down* R.

*Doric.* Do you—who? [*Crosses* R.

*Har.* My Letty.

*Doric.* O, I understand your rebuke! 'Tis too soon, sir, to assume the father-in-law. [*Crosses* L. H.

*Har.* Zounds! What do you mean by that? I tell you that the lady you admire is Letitia Hardy.

*Doric.* I am glad you are so well satisfied with the state of my heart—I wish I was! [*Exit* L. H.

*Har.* Stop a moment. Stop, I say! What! you won't? Very well—if I don't play you a trick for this, may I never be a grandfather to little Jeremiah! I'll plot with Letty now, and not against her; ay, hang me if I don't! There's something in my head that shall tingle in his heart. He shall have a lecture upon impatience that I foresee he'll be the better for as long as he lives. [*Rally of dancers, who jostle* HARDY.

[CURTAIN.]

43

# ACT III.

*Enter* Hardy *and* Villiers, R. H. I E.

*Vil.* Whimsical enough! Dying for her, and hates her! Believes her a fool, and a woman of brilliant understanding!

*Har.* As true as you are alive—but when I went up to him, last night, at the Pantheon, out of downright good nature, to explain things, my gentleman whips round upon his heel, and snapped me as short as if I had been a beggar woman with six children, and he overseer of the parish.

*Vil.* Here comes the wonder worker.

*Enter* Letitia, L. H. I E.

Here comes the enchantress, who can go to masquerades, and sing, and dance, and talk a man out of his wits! But, pray, have we morning masquerades?

*Let.* O no; but I am so enamoured of this all-conquering habit, that I could not resist putting it on the moment I had breakfasted. I shall wear it on the day I am married, and then lay it by in spices—like the miraculous robes of Saint Bridget.

*Vil.* That's as most brides do. The charms that helped to catch the husband are generally laid by, one after another, till the lady grows a downright wife, and then runs crying to her mother, because she has transformed her lover into a downright husband.

*Har.* Listen to me. I hain't slept to-night for thinking of plots to plague Doricourt; and they drove one another out of my head so quick that I was as giddy as a goose, and could

44

make nothing of them.    I wish to goodness you could contrive
something.                                                     [*Crosses* L.

*Vil.* [*Crosses to her.*]    Contrive to plague him!    Nothing
so easy.    Don't undeceive him, madam, till he is your husband.    Marry him while he possesses the sentiments you
labored to give him of Miss Hardy—and when you are his
wife——

*Let.* O, heavens!    I see the whole—that's the very thing.
My dear Mr. Villiers, you are the divinest man!

*Vil.* Don't make love to me, hussy.    [*Crosses* L. *of* LETITIA.


*Enter* MRS. RACKETT, L. H. I E.


*Mrs. R.* No, pray don't—for I design to have Villiers myself in
about six years.    [VILLIERS *goes* L.]    There's an oddity in him
that pleases me.    He holds women in contempt; and I should
like to have an opportunity of breaking his heart for that.

*Vil.* And when I am heartily tired of life, I know no woman
whom I would with more pleasure make my executioner.

*Har.* It cannot be.    [*Crosses* C.]    I foresee it will be impossible to bring it about.    You know the wedding wasn't to
take place this week or more ; and Letty will never be able to
play the fool so long.

*Vil.* [*Crosses between.*]    The knot shall be tied to-night.    I
have it all here—[*Pointing to his forehead.*]—the license is
ready.    Feign yourself ill ; send for Doricourt, and tell him you
can't go out of the world in peace, except you see the cere-
mony performed.

*Har.* I feign myself ill!    I could as soon feign myself a
Roman ambassador.    I was never ill in my life but with the
toothache—when Letty's mother was a-breeding.

*Vil.* O, I have no fears for you.    But what says Miss
Hardy?    Are you willing to make the irrevocable vow before
night?   [*Crosses to her.*]

*Let.* O, Heavens!    I—— 'Tis so exceeding sudden that
really——

*Mrs. R.* That really she is frightened out of her wits, lest it should be impossible to bring matters about. But I have taken the scheme into my protection, and you shall be Mrs. Doricourt before night. Come [*To* HARDY.] to bed directly ; your room shall be crammed with vials, and all the apparatus of death ; then, heigh, presto ! for Doricourt.

*Har.* Yes—but I'm not to take any physic.

*Vil.* You go and put off your conquering dress, and get all your awkward airs ready. And you practise a few groans— [*Crosses to* HARDY.]—and you, if possible, an air of gravity [*To* MRS. RACKETT]. I'll answer for the plot.

*Let.* Married in jest ! 'Tis an odd idea ! Well, I'll venture it. [*Exeunt* LETITIA *and* MRS. RACKETT, L. S.

*Vil.* Ay, I'll be sworn ! [*Looks at his watch.*] 'Tis past three. The Budget's to be opened this morning. I'll just step down to the House. Will you go ?

*Har.* What !—with a mortal sickness ?

*Vil.* What a blockhead ! I believe if half of us were to stay away with mortal sicknesses it would be for the health of the nation. Good-morning. I'll call and feel your pulse as I come back. [*Exit* L. H. I E.

*Har.* You won't find them over brisk, I fancy. I foresee some ill-happening from this making-believe die before one's time. But hang it—ahem ! I am a stout man yet ; only fifty-six. What's that ? In the last yearly bills there were three lived to above a hundred. Fifty-six ! Fiddle-de-dee ! I am not afraid, not I. [*Exit* R. H. I E.

———

SCENE 2.—2 G. DORICOURT'S *Lodgings as in Act I. Sofa*, C. *Table and chairs on* L. H. DORICOURT *discovered in his robe de chambre.*

*Enter* SAVILLE, L. H. I E.

*Sav.* Undressed so late ?

*Doric.* I didn't go to bed till late ; 'twas late before I slept —late when I rose. Do you know Lord George Jennett?

*Sav.* Yes.

*Doric.* Do you know the lady he loves!      [*Rises.*

*Sav.* Yes.

*Doric.* What sort of a creature is she ?

*Sav.* Why, she spends him three thousand a year with the ease of a duchess, and entertains his friends with the grace of a Ninon. [DORICOURT *walks about disordered.*] In the name of caprice, what ails you ?

*Doric.* [R.] You have hit it. *Elle est mon caprice.* The sweetheart of Lord George Jennett is my caprice. O, insufferable !

*Sav.* What, you saw her at the masquerade ?

*Doric.* Saw her—loved her—died for her, without knowing her ; and now, the curse is, I can't hate her.      [*Crosses* L.

*Sav.* Heyday! This sounds like love. What becomes of poor Miss Hardy ?

*Doric.* Her name has given me an ague ! Dear Saville, how shall I contrive to make old Hardy cancel the engagement ? The moiety of the estate, which he will forfeit, shall be his the next moment by deed of gift.

*Sav.* Let me see. Can't you get it insinuated that you are a devilish wild fellow ; that you are an infidel, and attached to fast living, gaming, and so forth ?

*Doric.* Ay, such a character might have done some good two centuries back. But who the deuce can it frighten now ? I believe it must be the mad scheme at last. There, will that do for a grin ?      [*Affects madness. Crosses* R.

*Sav.* Enough ; I have other news for you. Poor Hardy is confined to his bed ; they say he is going out of the world by the first post, and he wants to give you his blessing.

*Doric.* Ill! so ill ! I am sorry from my soul. He's a worthy little fellow—if he had not the gift of foreseeing so strongly.

*Sav.* Well, you must go and take leave.

*Doric.* What ?—to act the lunatic in the dying man's chamber ?

*Sav.* Exactly the thing ; and will bring your business to a short issue ; for his last commands must be that you are not to marry his daughter.

*Doric.* That's true, by Jupiter! and yet, hang it, impose upon a fellow at so serious a moment!—I can't do it.

[*Crosses* L. H.

*Sav.* You must, faith. I am answerable for your appearance, though it should be in a straight waistcoat. He knows your situation, and seems the more desirous of an interview.

*Doric.* I don't like encountering Rackett. She's an arch devil, and will discover the cheat.

*Sav.* There's a fellow!—cheated ninety-nine women, and now afraid of the hundredth.

*Doric.* And with reason; for that hundredth is a widow.

*Sav.* Ridiculous! But how became you certain that the lady you met at the masquerade is Lord George Jennett's enchantress?

*Doric.* Flutter told me so.

*Sav.* Then fifty to one against the intelligence.

*Doric.* It must be so. For there was a mystery in her air and manner for which nothing else can account. [*A violent rap heard.*] Who can this be?

*Sav.* [*Crosses. Looks out.*] The proverb is your answer— 'tis Flutter himself. Tip him a scene of the madman, and see how it takes.

*Doric.* I will—a good way to send it about town. Shall it be of the melancholy kind, or the raving?

*Sav.* Rant!—rant! Here he comes.

*Doric.* Talk not to me, who can pull comets by the beard, and overset an island?

*Enter* FLUTTER, L.; *crosses* C.

There! This is he!—this is he who hath sent my poor soul, without coat or breeches, to be tossed about in ether, like a duck-feather! Villain, give me my soul again! [*Seizes him.*

*Flut.* Upon my soul, I haven't got your soul.

[DORICOURT *releases him, and crosses to* R. H. FLUTTER *exceedingly frightened.* DORICOURT *throws himself on a lounge, kicking his feet up and down.* FLUTTER *bends forward to look at him. He reverses his position with a sudden jerk, and lays the other way; then sits up and nurses the sofa pillow as a baby.*

*Sav.* O, Mr. Flutter, what a melancholy sight! I little thought to see my poor friend reduced to this.

*Flut.* Mercy defend me! What, is he mad?

*Sav.* You see how it is. A cursed Italian lady—jealousy—gave him a drug—[FLUTTER *crosses* C.]—and every full of the moon——

*Doric.* Moon! Who dares talk of the moon? The patroness of genius—the rectifier of wits—the—O, here she is! I feel her—she tugs at my brain—she's got it—she's got it—O!

[*Exit* R. H. I E.

*Flut.* Hang it! I think he's got it. Well, this is dreadful! Exceeding dreadful, I protest.

*Sav.* The worthy Miss Hardy—what a misfortune!

*Flut.* Ay, very true. Do they know it?

*Sav.* O, no; the paroxysm seized him but this morning.

*Flut.* Adieu! I can't stay. [*Going in great haste*, L. H.

*Sav.* But you must stay [*Holding him.*] and assist me; perhaps he'll return again in a moment; and when he is in this way, his strength is prodigious.

*Flut.* Can't, indeed; can't, upon my soul. [*Going* L. H.

*Sav.* Flutter—don't make a mistake now; remember 'tis Doricourt that's mad.

*Flut.* Yes—you mad.

*Sav.* No, no; Doricourt.

*Flut.* Egad, I'll say you are both mad, and then I can't mistake.

[*Exeunt* FLUTTER, L. H. I E., SAVILLE R. H. I E.; FLUT-
TER *returns* L. H., *and crosses to* I E. R. H.

*Flut.* I should like to have one more peep at the madman.

*Doric.* [*Without*, R. I E.] Bring me a pickled elephant.

[FLUTTER *runs off*, I E. L. H.

SCENE 3.—*Apartment at* HARDY'S.

*Enter* MRS. RACKETT *and* MISS OGLE, L. H. I E.

*Miss O.* [L. C.]   And so Miss Hardy is actually to be married to-night?

*Mrs. R.* [R. C.]   If her fate does not deceive her.   You are apprised of the scheme, and we hope it will succeed.

*Miss O.* [*Aside.*]   Deuce take her!—she's six years younger than I am.   [*To* MRS. RACKETT.]   Is Mr. Doricourt handsome?

*Mrs. R.*   Handsome, generous, young, and rich.   There's a husband for ye!   Isn't he worth pulling caps for?   [*Crosses* L.

*Miss O.* [*Aside.*]   I' my conscience, the widow speaks as though she'd give cap, ears, and all for him.   [*To* MRS. RACKETT.]   I wonder you didn't try to catch this wonderful man, Mrs. Rackett?

*Mrs. R.*   Really, Miss Ogle, I had not time.   Besides, when I marry, so many stout young fellows will hang themselves, that, out of regard to society, in these sad times, I shall postpone it for a few years.

*Enter* FLUTTER, L. H. I E., *in great perturbation.*

*Flut.*   Here they come!—here they come!   Their coach stopped as mine drove off.        [MISS OGLE *gets* R.

*Sav.* [*Without,* L. H.]   Come, let me guide you!   This way, my poor friend!   Why are you so furious?

*Doric.* [*Without,* L. H.]   The house of death—[FLUTTER *darts up out of the way in great alarm.*]—to the house of death!

*Enter* DORICOURT *and* SAVILLE, L. H. I E.   SAVILLE *tries to hold* DORICOURT *back by the coat tail.*

Ah! this is the spot!        [FLUTTER *rushes to* R. H. *corner.*

*Mrs. R.*   How wild and fiery he looks!

*Miss O.*   Now, I think he looks terrified!

*Mrs. R.* [*Advances toward him with pretended fear.*] I never saw a madman before. Let me examine him. Will he bite ?

[*As she gets near him he snorts and snarls. All start back.*

*Sav.* [*Crosses* C.] Pray keep out of his reach, ladies—you don't know your danger. He's like a wildcat, if a sudden thought seizes him.

*Mrs. R.* You talk like a keeper of wildcats. How much do you demand for showing the monster ?

*Doric.* [*Aside.*] I don't like this—I must rouse their sensibility. [*Crosses to* C., *dancing and waving his arms in an idiotic manner.*] There ! there she darts through the air in liquid flames. Now she's up, up, up ! Now she's down, down, down ! Down again—now I have her—O, she burns !—she scorches ! [*Clapping his hands to his temples.*] She swims into my brain ! [*Clutching at his breast.*] Now she eats, she eats into my very heart ! She's got it !—she's got it !

[*Falls into* SAVILLE'S *arms.*

*Omnes.* Ha, ha, ha !

*Flut.* [*Crosses* C.] Doricourt, give her highness a pinch.

*Doric.* I am laughed at !

*Mrs. R.* [C.] Laughed at ?—ay, to be sure. Why, I could play the madman better than you. There !—there she is ! Now I have her ! Ha, ha, ha ! Mr. Flutter, why don't you catch me ?

[*Falls into the arms of* FLUTTER, *who bends over and kisses her. She strikes him with her fan, and pursues him up stage.*

*Doric.* [*Down* R., *and up* C.] I'll leave the house ; I'm covered with confusion. [*Going* L. H.

*Mrs. R.* Stay, sir—you must not go. 'Twas poorly done, Mr. Doricourt, to affect madness rather than fulfil your engagements.

*Doric.* Affect madness ? [*Crosses* L.] Saville, what can I do ?

*Sav.* Since you are discovered, confess the whole.

*Doric.* Yes ; since my designs have been so unaccountably discovered, I will avow the whole. I cannot love Miss Hardy, and will never——

*Sav.* Hold, my dear Doricourt! What will the world say to such——

*Doric.* Hang the world! What will the world give me for the loss of happiness? Must I sacrifice my peace to please the world?

*Sav.* [*Crosses* R. C.] Yes, everything, rather than be branded with dishonor.

*Mrs. R.* [C.] Though our arguments should fail, there is a pleader whom you surely cannot withstand. *The dying Mr. Hardy* supplicates you not to forsake his child.

*Doric.* The dying Mr. Hardy!     [*Going slowly toward* R.
*Mrs. R.* The dying Mr. Hardy!
*Sav.* The dying Mr. Hardy!
*Miss O.* The dying Mr. Hardy!
*Flut.* The dying Mr. Hardy!

[*All repeat this from* R. H. *to* L. H.

When DORICOURT *gets to* R., *he meets* VILLIERS, *who enters* R. H. D. I E.

*Vil.* [*Crosses* L.] *The dying Mr. Hardy* [DORICOURT *takes stage back to* L.] requests you to grant him a moment's conversation, Mr. Doricourt, though you should persist to send him miserable to the grave. Let me conduct you to his chamber.                                                   [*Back to* R.

*Doric.* O, ay, anywhere; to the antipodes—to the moon—carry me. Do with me what you will.

[*Crosses hastily to* R. FLUTTER *flies out of the way and gets* L.

*Mrs. R.* I'll follow, and let you know what passes.

[*Exeunt* DORICOURT, MRS. RACKETT, *and* MISS OGLE, R. H., D. I E.

*Flut.* Ladies, ladies, have the charity to take me with you, that I may make no blunder in repeating the story.

[*Exit* R. H. D. I E.

*Sav.* [C.] Now for an answer to the great conundrum of the hour: who shall win? Will Letitia's nerve sustain her? Will old Hardy's counterfeit deceive the practised eye of our

traveller ?—or will Flutter's curiosity or Rackett's deviltry discover the whole plot, and turn our Belle's Stratagem to nought
after all ? [*A hubbub of voices is heard off.*

*Re-enter* MRS. RACKETT, MISS OGLE, *and* FLUTTER, R.H.D. I E.
*all interrupting each other.*

*Mrs. R.* [L. C.] O, do you know——-
*Flut.* [C.] Let me tell the story. As soon as Doricourt——
*Mrs. R.* I protest you shan't. Said Mr. Hardy——
*Flut.* No, 'twas Doricourt spoke first—says he—no, 'twas
the parson—says he—— [*Crosses to* SAVILLE.
*Mrs. R.* Stop his mouth, Saville; he'll spoil the tale.
*Sav.* Never heed the circumstances—the result—the result.
*Mrs. R.* [*Crosses to* SAVILLE.] No, no ; you shall have it in
form. Mr. Hardy performed the sick man like an angel. He
sat up in bed, and talked so pathetically, that the tears stood
in Doricourt's eyes.
*Flut.* [*Crosses.*] Ay, stood—they did not drop, but stood.
I shall in future be very exact ; the parson seized the moment ;
you know they never miss an opportunity.
*Mrs. R.* [*Crosses.*] " Make haste," said Doricourt ; "if I
have time to reflect, poor Hardy will die unhappy."
*Flut.* They were got as far as the day of judgment, when
we slipped out of the room.
*Mrs. R.* Here comes the bridegroom of to-night.

*Re-enter* DORICOURT *and* VILLIERS, R. H. D. I E. VILLIERS
*whispers to* SAVILLE, *who goes out,* L. H. I E.

*Omnes.* Joy ! joy ! joy !
[*Same business of crossing him as in dying scene.* DORI-
COURT *walks about in front.*
*Miss O.* If he's a sample of bridegrooms, keep me single !
A younger brother from the funeral of his father could not
carry a more fretful countenance.
*Flut.* O, now he's melancholy mad, I suppose.
*Mrs. R.* You do not consider the importance of the occasion.

*Vil.* [C.] No; nor how shocking a thing it is for a man to be forced to marry one woman while his heart is devoted to another. [*Down* R.

*Mrs. R.* [*Crosses to him.*] Well, now it's over, I confess to you, Mr. Doricourt, I think 'twas a most ridiculous piece of Quixotism, to give up the happiness of a whole life to a man who perhaps has but a few moments to be sensible of the sacrifice.

*Flut.* So it appeared to me. But, thought I, Mr. Doricourt has travelled—he knows best.

*Doric.* [*On* R. H.] Zounds! confusion!—[*Crossing angrily to* C. FLUTTER *goes up and across in alarm.*]—did ye not all set upon me! Didn't ye talk to me of honor—compassion—justice? [*Crossing.*] Heavens! to felicity I bid adieu, but I will endeavor to be content. Where is my—I choke as I speak the word—where is my—wife?

*Enter* LETITIA, L. U. E., *masked, led by* SAVILLE.

*Sav.* Mr. Doricourt, this lady was pressing to be introduced to you. [*Down* L.

*Doric.* [C., *starting.*] Oh!

*Let.* [L. C.] I told you last night you should see me at a time when you least expected me, and I have kept my promise.

*Vil.* Whoever you are, madam, you could not have arrived at a happier moment. Mr. Doricourt is just married.

*Let.* Married!—impossible! 'Tis but a few hours since he swore to me eternal love; I believed him, gave him up my virgin heart—and now!—Ungrateful sex!

*Doric.* Your virgin heart! No, lady—[FLUTTER *exhibits great uneasiness.*]—my fate, thank Heaven, yet wants that torture. Nothing but the conviction that you were another's could have made me think one moment of marriage, to have saved the lives of half mankind. But this visit, madam, is as barbarous as unexpected. It is now my duty to forget you, which, spite of your situation, I found difficult enough.

*Let.* My situation! What situation?

*Doric.* I must apologize for explaining it in this company—but, madam, I am not ignorant that Lord George Jennett has a better claim than I upon your heart—and this is the only circumstance that can give me peace.

*Let.* I!—Sir George!—ridiculous pretence! No, sir; know, to your confusion, that my heart, my honor, my name, is unspotted as hers you have married; my birth equal to your own, my fortune large. That, and my person, might have been yours. But, sir, farewell! [*Going* L. H.

*Doric.* O, stay a moment. [*Flies at* FLUTTER, *who retreats* C.] Rascal!—is she not——

*Flut.* No! 'pon my soul, she's not. Who, she? O, Lord! —no. 'Twas quite a different person that I meant. I never saw that lady before.

*Doric.* Then, never shalt thou see her again.

[*Shakes* FLUTTER, *throws him off; he staggers over to* MRS. RACKETT *and* MISS OGLE, *who fan him, one on each side.*

*Mrs. R.* Have mercy upon the poor man! Heavens, he'll murder him.

*Doric.* Murder him! Yes, you, myself, and all mankind. [*Crosses in front* R. *and* L.] Saville, Villiers—'twas you who pushed me on this precipice; 'tis you who have snatched from me joy, felicity, and life!

*Mrs. R.* There! now, how well he acts the madman! This is something like! I knew he would do it well enough when the time came.

*Doric.* Hard-hearted woman! enjoy my ruin—riot in my wretchedness.


*Enter* HARDY, *hastily in his nightcap and gown, and face covered with flour*, R. H. I E.


*Har.* This is too much. You are now the husband of my daughter; and how dare you show all this passion about another woman?

*Doric.* Alive again!

*Har.* Alive! ay, and merry. Here! wipe off the flour from

my face. I was never in better health and spirits in all my life. I foresaw 'twould do. Why, my illness was only a fetch, man, to make you marry Letty. [*Crosses to* DORICOURT.

*Doric.* It was? Base and ungenerous! Well, sir, you shall be gratified. The possession of my heart was no object either with you or your daughter. My fortune and name were all you desired, and these—I leave ye. My native country I shall quit, nor never behold you more. But, lady—[*Crosses to her.*]—that in my exile I may have one consolation, grant me the favor you denied last night: let me behold all that mask conceals, that your whole image may be impressed on my heart, and cheer my distant solitary hours.

*Let.* This is the most awful moment of my life. O, Doricourt, the slight action of taking off my mask, stamps me the most blest, or miserable of women!

*Doric.* What can this mean? Reveal your face, I conjure you.

*Let.* [C.] Behold it. [*Unmasks.*

*Doric.* [C.] Rapture! transport! heaven!

*Flut.* Now he's got it again. Now for a touch of the happy madman.

*Let.* This little stratagem arose from my disappointment in not having made the impression on you I wished. The timidity of the English character threw a veil over me you could not penetrate. You have forced me to emerge in some measure from my natural reserve, and to throw off the veil that hid me.

*Doric.* Speak on, sweet angel!

*Har.* The dog! how well he makes up for past slights! Cousin Rackett, I wish you a good husband, with all my heart. Mr. Flutter, I'll believe every word you say this fortnight— though I foresee I'll have to swallow a lot of salt with what you say. Mr. Villiers, you and I have managed this to a T. I never was so merry in my life. 'Gad, I believe I can dance. [*Footing.*

*Doric.* Charming, charming creature!

*Let.* Congratulate me, my dear friends! Can you conceive my happiness?

*Har.* No, congratulate me, for mine is the greatest.

*Flut.* [*Crosses, and back.*] No, congratulate me, that I have escaped with life, and give me some sticking-plaster—that wildcat has torn the skin from my throat.

*Har.* Come into the next room; I have ordered out every drop of my forty-eight, and I'll invite the whole parish of St. George's but we'll drink it out—except one dozen, which I shall keep under three double locks, for the christening of little Jeremiah, that I foresee will happen within this twelvemonth.

*Doric.* My charming bride!

*Let.* But this my stratagem proves from youth to age,
All wear the mask. Here only on the stage
You see us as we are: Here trust your eyes.
Our wish to please—we never here disguise.

CURTAIN.

# THE WONDER!

# A WOMAN KEEPS A SECRET

A COMEDY BY MRS. CENTLIVRE

*ARRANGED IN FOUR ACTS*

BY

AUGUSTIN DALY

As Produced at Daly's Theatre, New York

1893
Privately Printed for Mr. Daly

# CAST OF CHARACTERS.

| | Drury Lane, London. | Federal Street, Boston, 1828. | Howard Athenæum, Boston, 1846. | Federal Street, Boston, 1846. | Daly's Theatre, New York. |
|---|---|---|---|---|---|
| DON FELIX.............. | Mr. Elliston. | Mr. H. J. Finn. | Mr. G. Vandenhoff. | Mr. J. Wallack. | Creston Clarke. |
| COLONEL BRITON........ | Mr. Holland. | Mr. Bernard. | Mr. J. H. Hall. | Mr. H. W. Bland. | George Clarke. |
| FREDERIC.............. | Mr. Barnard. | Mr. Jones, | Mr. Bradshaw. | Mr. R. Stephens. | Sidney Herbert. |
| DON PEDRO............. | Mr. Gattie. | Mr. Kilner. | Mr. C. H. Saunders. | Mr. J. G. Gilbert. | Charles Wheatleigh. |
| DON LOPEZ............. | Mr. Hughes, | Mr. Clarke. | Mr. C. L. Stone. | Mr. S. D. Johnson. | Charles Leclercq. |
| GIBBY ................ | Mr. Palmer. | Mr. Bancker. | Mr. Chippendale. | Mr. D. Whiting. | William Gilbert. |
| LISSARDO............. | Mr. Harley. | Mr. G. H. Andrews. | Mr. Warren. | Mr. T. Placide. | James Lewis. |
| VASQUEZ.............. | Mr. Evans. | Mr. Osborne. | ........ | Mr. Adams. | William Sampson. |
| ALGUAZIL............. | Mr. Maddocks. | Mr. Tryon. | ........ | ........ | George Wharnock. |
| SERVANT ............. | Mr Minton. | Mr. Adams. | Mr. Parsons. | Mr. Parsons. | Edward Wilks. |
| DONNA VIOLANTE....... | Mrs. Glover. | Miss Placide. | Mrs. W. H. Crisp. | Mrs. H. W. Bland. | Ada Rehan. |
| DONNA ISABELLA....... | Mrs. Orger. | Mrs. Bernard. | Miss Maywood. | Miss Wagstaff. | Adelaide Prince. |
| FLORA................ | Miss Kelley. | Mrs. Kilner. | Miss M. Taylor. | Miss Roquet. | Kitty Cheatham. |
| INIS ................ | Mrs. Scott. | Mrs. Bernard. | Mrs. E. Eddy. | Mrs. W. H. Smith. | Lucie Celeste. |

3

# THE WONDER!

## ACT I.

SCENE I.—*A Street*, I G.

*Enter* DON LOPEZ, L. H. I E., *meeting* FREDERIC, R. II. I E.

*Fred.* My Lord, Don Lopez.

*Lop.* How d'ye, Frederic?

*Fred.* At your lordship's service. I am glad to see you look so well, my lord; I hope Antonio's out of danger.

*Lop.* Quite the contrary; his fever increases, they tell me; and the surgeons are of opinion his wound is mortal.

*Fred.* Your son, Don Felix, is safe, I hope.

*Lop.* I hope so, too; but they offer large rewards to apprehend him.

*Fred.* When heard your lordship from him?

*Lop.* Not since he went. I forbade him writing till the public news gave him an account of Antonio's health; for I intend to marry my daughter to Don Guzman, whom I expect from Holland every day, whither he went to take possession of a large estate left him by his uncle.     [*Crosses* R.

*Fred.* You will not, surely, sacrifice the lovely Isabella to age, avarice, and a fool? Pardon the expression, my lord; but my concern for your beauteous daughter transports me beyond that good manners which I ought to pay to your lordship's presence.

*Lop.* I can't deny the justness of the character, Frederic; but I resolve she shall marry Don Guzman the moment he

5

arrives. [*Crosses to* R. H.] Though I could not govern my son, I will my daughter, I assure you.

*Fred.* This match, my lord, is more preposterous than that which you proposed to your son, from whence arose this fatal quarrel. Don Antonio's sister, Elvira, wanted beauty only; but Guzman everything but——

*Lop.* Money, and that will purchase everything; and so adieu. [*Exit* R. H.

*Fred.* Monstrous! These are the resolutions which destroy the comforts of matrimony——

*Enter* LISSARDO, L. H. I E., *in a riding habit.*

Lissardo! from whence came you?

*Lis.* That letter will inform you, sir.

*Fred.* I hope your master's safe.

*Lis.* I left him so; I have another to deliver which requires haste. Your most humble servant, sir.

[*Bowing, crosses to* R. H.

*Fred.* To Violante, I suppose.

*Lis.* The same. [*Exit* R. H. I E.

*Fred.* [*Reads:*] "*Dear Frederic—the two chief blessings of this life are, a friend and a mistress; to be debarred the sight of those is not to live. I hear nothing of Antonio's death, and therefore resolve to venture to thy house this evening, impatient to see Violante, and embrace my friend. Yours,* FELIX." Pray heaven he comes undiscovered.—Ha! Colonel Briton.

*Enter* COLONEL BRITON, R. H. I E.

*Col. B.* Frederic, I rejoice to see thee.

*Fred.* What brought you to Lisbon, Colonel?

*Col. B.* "La fortune de la guerre," as the French say.

*Fred.* If you are not provided of a lodging, Colonel, pray command my house while you stay.

*Col. B.* If I were sure I should not be troublesome I would accept your offer, Frederic.

*Fred.* So far from trouble, Colonel, I shall take it as a particular favor. What have we here?

*Col. B.* My footman. This is our country dress, you must know, which, for the honor of Scotland, I make all my servants wear.

*Enter* GIBBY, *in a Highland dress,* R. H. I E.

*Gibby.* What mun I de with the horses, and like yer honor? [*Crosses* C.] They will tak cold gin they stand in the causeway.]
*Fred.* O, I'll take care of them. What, hoa! Vasquez!

*Enter* VASQUEZ, R. H. I E.

Put the horses, which that honest fellow will show you, into my stable; do you hear? and feed them well.
*Vas.* Yes, sir. [VASQUEZ *crosses to* GIBBY, *and bows to him.*] Sir, by my master's orders, I am, sir, your most obsequious, humble servant. Be pleased to lead the way.
*Gibby.* 'Sbleed, gang yer gate, sir, and I sall follow ye. [VASQUEZ *goes* L.] I'se tee hungry to feed on compliments.
[*Exit* L. I E. H., VASQUEZ *bowing him off.*
*Fred.* Ha, ha! a comical fellow. Well, how do you like our country, Colonel?
*Col. B.* Why, faith, Frederic, a man might pass his time agreeably enough; but to behold such troops of soft, plump, tender, melting girls, through a confounded grating, gives us Britons strong temptations to plunder! Wilt thou recommend me to a wife—ha, friend!
*Fred.* She must be very handsome, I suppose?
*Col. B.* The handsomer the better—but be sure she has a nose.
*Fred.* Ay, ay, and some gold.
*Col. B.* O, very much gold; I shall never be able to swallow the matrimonial pill if it be not well gilded. [*Crosses* R.
*Fred.* Pho; beauty will make it slide down nimbly.
*Col. B.* At first, perhaps, it may. I confess, Frederic, women are the prettiest playthings in nature; but gold, substantial gold, gives 'em the air, the mien, the shape, the grace, and beauty of a goddess.

7

*Fred.* And has⁻ not gold the same ⁻divinity in their eyes, Colonel ?

*Col. B.* Too often——

> None marry now for love ; that's a jest at least
> The self-same bargain serves for wife and beast.

> *[Crosses* L.

*Fred.* You are always gay, Colonel.   Come, shall we take a refreshing glass at my house, and consider what has been said ?

*Col. B.* I have two or three compliments to discharge for some friends, and then I shall wait on you with pleasure.   In the close of the evening I will endeavor to kiss your hand. Adieu.

*Fred.* I shall expect you with impatience.

> *[Exeunt* COLONEL, L. H. I E., *and* FREDERIC, R. H. I E.

————

SCENE 2.—*A Room in* DON LOPEZ'S *House.*

*Enter* ISABELLA, *followed by* INIS, *her maid,* R. H. 2 E.

*Inis.* For goodness' sake, madam, where are you going in this pet ?

*Isa.* Anywhere, to avoid matrimony : the thought of a husband is terrible to me.

*Inis.* Ay, of an old husband ; but if you may choose for yourself, I fancy matrimony would be no such frightful thing to you.

*Isa.* You are pretty much in the right, Inis ; but to be forced into the arms of an idiot, who has neither person to please the eye, sense to charm the ear, nor generosity to supply those defects !   I must contrive some way to avoid Don Guzman, and yet stay in my own country.

*Enter* DON LOPEZ, L. H. I E.

*Lop.* Must you so, mistress ? but I shall take care to prevent you. *[Aside.]* Isabella, whither are you going, my child ?

*Isa.* To church, sir.

8

*Inis.* [*Aside.*] The old rogue has certainly overheard her.

*Lop.* Your devotion must needs be very strong, or your memory very weak, my dear ; why, vespers are over for this night. Come, come, you shall have a better errand to church than to say your prayers there. Don Guzman is arrived in the river, and I expect him ashore to-morrow.

*Isa.* Ha ! To-morrow!

*Lop.* He writes me word that his estate in Holland is worth twelve thousand crowns a year, which, together with what he had before, will make thee the happiest wife in Lisbon.

*Isa.* And the most unhappy woman in the world. [ *Taking his hand.*] O, sir, if I have any power in your heart, if the tenderness of a father be not quite extinct, hear me with patience.

*Lop.* No objection against the marriage, and I will hear whatsoever thou hast to say. Remember, 'tis your duty to obey.

*Isa.* I never disobeyed before, and wish I had not reason now ; but nature has got the better of my duty, and makes me loathe the harsh commands you lay.

*Lop.* Ha, ha! very fine ! Ha, ha!

*Isa.* Death itself would be welcome ! [*Crosses* L.

*Lop.* Are you sure of that ?

*Isa.* I am your daughter, my lord, and can boast as strong a resolution as yourself; I'll die before I'll marry Guzman !

*Lop.* Say you so ? I'll try that presently. [*Draws.*] Here, let me see with what dexterity you can breathe a vein now. [*Offers her his sword.*] The point is pretty sharp ; 'twill do your business, I warrant you.

*Inis.* [*Going between them.*] Bless me, sir, what do you mean, to put a sword into the hands of a desperate woman ?

*Lop.* Desperate ! ha, ha, ha ! you see how desperate she is. What! art thou frighted, little Belle—ha ?

*Isa.* I confess I am startled at your morals, sir.

*Lop.* Ay, ay, child, thou hadst better take the man.

*Isa.* I shall take neither, sir ; [*Crosses* C.] death has many doors ; and when I can live no longer with pleasure, I shall find one to let him in at without your aid.

9

*Lop.* Sayest thou so, my dear Belle? Ods, I'm afraid thou art a little lunatic, Belle. I must take care of thee, child. [*Takes hold of her, and pulls a key out of his pocket.*] I shall make bold to secure thee, my dear. I'll see if locks and bars can keep thee till Guzman comes. Go, get into your chamber.
[*Pushes her in, and locks flat.*

There I'll your boasted resolution try—
And see who'll get the better, you or I.
[*As he locks* ISABELLA *in closet,* INIS *follows close behind him. As he advances to speak his couplet, she taps on the door. He hears her, runs after her—catches her by the nape of the neck, aud runs her off.*]

———

SCENE 3.—*Handsome apartment at* DON PEDRO'S. *Large window,* C. *Doors,* R. *and* L.

*Enter* VIOLANTE, *reading a letter, and* FLORA, *following,*
D. R. H. I E.

*Flora.* What! must that letter be read again?
*Vio.* Yes, and again, and again, and again, a thousand times again; a letter from a faithful lover can never be read too often: it speaks such kind, such soft, such tender things.
[*Crosses* R. *Sits. Kisses it.*
*Flora.* But always the same language.
*Vio.* It does not charm the less for that. [*Reads:*] " *My all that's charming, since life's not life, exiled from thee, this night shall bring me to thy arms. Frederic and thee are all I trust. This six weeks' absence has been, in love's account, six hundred years. When it is dark, expect the wonted signal at thy window; till when, adieu. Thine, more than his own.*
" FELIX."
*Flora.* [*Aside.*] Who would not have said as much to a lady of her beauty, and twenty thousand pounds?—Were I a man, methinks I could have said a hundred finer things.
*Vio.* What would you have said?

*Flora.* I would have compared your eyes to the stars, your teeth to ivory, your lips to coral, your neck to alabaster, your shape to——

*Vio.* No more of your bombast; truth is the best eloquence in a lover. [*Rises.*] What proof remains ungiven of his love? When his father threatened to disinherit him for refusing Don Antonio's sister, from whence sprang this unhappy quarrel, did it shake his love for me? And now, though strict inquiry runs through every place, with large rewards to apprehend him, does he not venture all for me? [*Crosses* L.

*Flora.* But you know, madam, your father, Don Pedro, designs you for a nun,—to be sure you look very like a nun,—and says your grandfather left you your fortune upon that condition.

*Vio.* Not without my approbation, girl, when I come to one and twenty, as I am informed. But, however, I shall run the risk of that. Go, call in Lissardo. [*Sits* R.

*Flora.* Yes, madam. [*Aside.*] Now for a thousand verbal questions.

[*Goes to door, and beckons to* LISSARDO, *who enters.*

*Vio.* [R. H.] Well, and how do you, Lissardo?

*Lis.* [C.] Ah, very weary, madam. [*Apart to* FLORA.] Faith, thou look'st wondrous pretty, Flora.

*Flora.* [*Apart to* LISSARDO.] You'd make one believe you are wondrous fond now.

*Vio.* Where did you leave your master?

*Lis.* [*Apart to* FLORA.] Odd, if I had you alone, I'd show you how fond I could be!

*Vio.* Where did you leave your master?

*Lis.* At a little farm house, madam, about five miles off. He'll be at Don Frederic's in the evening.

[*Apart to* FLORA.]
Odd, I will so revenge myself of those lips of thine.

*Vio.* Is he in health?

*Flora.* [L. H., *apart to* LISSARDO.] O, you counterfeit wondrous well.

*Lis.* [*Apart to* FLORA.] No; every body knows I counterfeit very ill.

*Vio.* [*Rises and comes forward.*] How say you? Is Felix ill? What's his distemper—ha?

*Lis.* [C.] Love, madam, love. In short, madam, I believe he has thought of nothing but your ladyship ever since he left Lisbon. I am sure he could not, if I may judge of his heart by my own.                    [*Looks lovingly upon* FLORA.

*Vio.* How came you so well acquainted with your master's thoughts, Lissardo?

*Lis.* By an infallible rule, madam, words are the pictures of the mind, you know ; now, to prove he thinks of nothing but you, he talks of nothing but you—for example, madam, coming from shooting t'other day, with a brace of partridges, "Lissardo," said he, "go bid the cook roast me this brace of Violantes." [*To* FLORA.] I flew into the kitchen, full of thoughts of thee, and cried, " Here, cook, roast me this brace of Florellas."

*Flora.* [*To* LISSARDO.] Ha, ha! Excellent! You mimic your master, then, it seems.

*Lis.* Another time, madam, the priest came to make him a visit ; he called out hastily : " Lissardo," said he, " bring a Violante for my father to sit down on." Then he often mistook my name, madam, and called me Violante ; in short, I heard it so often that it became as familiar to me as my prayers.

*Vio.* You live very merrily, then, it seems.

*Lis.* O, exceeding merry, madam.    [*Kisses* FLORA'S *hand.*

*Vio.* Ha! exceeding merry? Had you treats and balls?

*Lis.* O, yes, yes, madam, several.

*Flora.* [*Apart to* LISSARDO.] You are mad, Lissardo ; you don't mind what my lady says to you.

*Vio.* [*Aside.*] Ha! balls? Is he so merry in my absence? And did your master dance, Lissardo?

*Lis.* Dance, madam! Where, madam?

*Vio.* Why, at those balls you speak of.

*Lis.* Balls! What balls, madam?

*Vio.* Why, sure you are in love, Lissardo. Did not you say, but now, you had balls where you have been?

*Lis.* Balls, madam! What balls, ma'am? Odslife, I ask your

pardon, madam! I—I—I had mislaid some wash-balls of my master's t'other day; and because I could not think where I had laid them, just when he asked for them, he very fairly broke my head, madam; and now it seems I can think of nothing else. Alas! he dance, madam? No, no, poor gentleman, he is as melancholy as an unbraced drum.

*Vio.* Poor Felix! There, wear that ring for your master's sake, and let him know I shall be ready to receive him.
[*Exit* D. R. H. I E.

*Lis.* I shall, madam. [*Puts on the ring.*] Methinks a diamond ring is a vast addition to the little finger of a gentleman.
[*Admires his hand.*

*Flora.* [*Aside.*] That ring must be mine.—Well, Lissardo, what haste you make to pay off arrears now! Look how the fellow stands!

*Lis.* Egad, methinks I have a very pretty hand [*Crosses* L.] —and very white—and the shape! Faith, I never minded it so much before! In my opinion, it is a very fine-shaped hand, and becomes a diamond ring as well as the first grandee's in Portugal.

*Flora.* The man's transported! Is this your love? This your impatience?

*Lis.* [*Takes snuff.*] Now, in my mind, I take snuff with a very jantee air. [*Struts across* R.

*Flora.* Sweet Mr. Lissardo—[*Courtesies.*]—if I may presume to speak to you without affronting your little finger——

*Lis.* Odso, madam, I ask your pardon. Is it to me or to the ring you direct your discourse, madam?
[*Up and across* L.

*Flora.* Madam, good lack! How much a diamond ring improves one!

*Lis.* Why, though I say it, I can carry myself as well as anybody. [*Down.*] But what wert you going to say, child?

*Flora.* Why, I was going to say—that I fancy you had best let me keep that ring; it will be a very pretty wedding-ring, Lissardo; would it not?

*Lis.* Humph! —ah! — but — but—but—I believe I shan't marry yet awhile. [*Crosses* R.

*Flora.* You shan't, you say? Very well! I suppose you design that ring for Inis?

*Lis.* No, no; I never bribe an old acquaintance. Perhaps I might let it sparkle in the eyes of a stranger a little, till we come to a right understanding—but, then, like all other mortal things, it would return from whence it came.

*Flora.* Insolent! Is that your manner of dealing?

*Lis.* With all but thee.—Kiss me, you little rogue you.

[*Hugs her, and turns her* R.

*Flora.* Little rogue! Pr'ythee, fellow, don't be so familiar. [*Pushes him away.*] If I mayn't keep your ring, I can keep my kisses.

*Lis.* You can, you say? Spoke with the air of a chambermaid.

*Flora.* Replied with the spirit of a serving man.

*Re-enter* VIOLANTE, R. U. E.

*Lis.* [L. C.] Pr'ythee, Flora, don't let you and I fall out; I am in a merry humor, and shall certainly fall in somewhere.

*Flora.* What care I where you fall in!

*Vio.* [R.] Why do you keep Lissardo so long, Flora, when you don't know how soon my father may awake? His afternoon naps are never long.

*Flora.* [*Aside.*] Had Don Felix been with her, she would not have thought the time long. These ladies consider nobody's wants but their own.

*Vio.* Go, go, let him out.

[FLORA *goes up to table and gets candle.*

*Flora.* Yes, madam.

*Lis.* I fly, madam. [*Exeunt* LISSARDO *and* FLORA, L. U. E.

*Vio.* The day draws in, and night, the lover's friend, advances—night, more welcome than the sun to me, because it brings my love.

*Flora.* [*Within,* I E. L. H.] Ah, thieves, thieves! murder, murder!

*Vio.* [*Shrieks.*] Ah, what do I hear? Felix is certainly pursued, and will be taken.

*Re-enter* FLORA, *with a broken candle in candlestick, running,*
L. U. E.

How now! Answer me quickly; what's the matter?

*Flora.* O madam, as I was letting out Lissardo, a gentleman rushed between him and me, struck down my candle, and is bringing a dead person in his arms into our house.

*Vio.* A dead person! Heaven grant it does not prove my Felix.

*Flora.* Here they are, madam.

*Vio.* I'll retire till you discover the meaning of this accident.
[*Exit*, R. U. E.  FLORA *places chair*, C.

*Enter* COLONEL BRITON, D. L. H. I E., *with* ISABELLA *in his arms, whom he sits down in a chair, and addresses himself to* FLORA.

*Col. B.* [L.] Madam, the necessity this lady was under of being conveyed into some house with speed and secrecy, will, I hope, excuse any indecency I might be guilty of in pressing so rudely into this—I am an entire stranger to her name and circumstances. I commit her, madam, to your care, and fly to make her retreat secure; if the street be clear, permit me to return, and learn from her own mouth if I can be further serviceable. Pray, madam, what is the lady of this house called?

*Flora.* Violante, seignior.

*Col. B.* Are you she, madam?

*Flora.* Only her woman, seignior.

*Col. B.* Your humble servant, mistress. Pray be careful of the lady.
[*In taking out his handkerchief to get at his purse, drops a letter and exits.*

*Flora.* Two moidores! Well, he is a generous fellow. This is the only way to make one careful. I see these military rules are just the same in every country. They understand the constitution of the chambermaid.
[*Gets* L. *of chair.*

*Re-enter* VIOLANTE, D. R. H. I E.

*Vio.* [R.] Was you distracted, Flora, to tell my name to a man you never saw ? Unthinking wench ! Who knows what this may turn to ? What, is the lady dead ? Ah, Heaven ! 'tis Isabella, sister to my Felix. What has befallen her ? Pray Heaven he's safe. Run and fetch some cold water. Stay, stay, Flora—Isabella, friend, speak to me—O, speak to me.

*Isa.* O, hold, dear father, do not force me. Indeed I cannot love him.

*Vio.* How wild she talks !

*Isa.* Where am I ? [*Rises.*

*Vio.* With one as sensible of thy pain as thou thyself canst be.

*Isa.* Violante ! what kind star preserved and lodged me here ?

*Flora.* It was a terrestrial star, called a man, madam ; pray Jupiter he proves a lucky one.

*Isa.* O, I remember now. Forgive me, dear Violante ; my thoughts ran so much upon the danger I escaped, I forgot.
[*All down.*

*Vio.* May I not know your story ?

*Isa.* Thou art no stranger to one part of it. I have often told thee that my father designed to sacrifice me to Don Guzman, who, it seems, is just returned from Holland. Upon my refusing to obey him, he locked me into my chamber, vowing to keep me there till he arrived, and force me to consent. I know my father to be positive, never to be won from his design ; and having no hope left me to escape the marriage, I leaped from the window into the street. [*Crosses* R.

*Vio.* You have not hurt yourself, I hope.

*Isa.* No ; a gentleman passing by, by accident, caught me in his arms : at first, my fright made me apprehend it was my father, till he assured me to the contrary.

*Flora.* He is a very fine gentleman, I promise you, madam; and a well-bred man, I warrant him. I think I never saw a grandee put his hand into his pocket with a better air in my whole lifetime ; then he opened his purse with such a grace, that nothing but his manner of presenting me with the gold could equal.

*Vio.* Go, leave us, Flora. [*Exit* FLORA, L. U. E.] But how came you hither, Isabella ?

*Isa.* I know not ; I desired the stranger to convey me to the next monastery ; but erè I reached the door, I saw, or fancied that I saw, Lissardo, my brother's man ; and the thought that his master might not be far off, flung me into a swoon, which is all that I can remember. [*Crosses* C.] Ha ! what's here ? [*Picks up letter on stage.*] " For Colonel Briton. To be left at the post-house in Lisbon." This must be dropped by the stranger who brought me hither.

*Vio.* Thou art fallen into the hands of a soldier ; take care he does not lay thee under contribution, girl. [*Rises.*

*Isa.* I find he is a gentleman ; and if he is but unmarried, I could be content to follow him all the world over. But I shall never see him more, I fear. [*Sits* L. *Sighs, and pauses.*

*Vio.* What makes you sigh, Isabella ?

*Isa.* The fear of falling into my father's clutches again.

*Vio.* Can I be serviceable to you ?

*Isa.* [*Rises.*] Yes, if you conceal me two or three days.

*Vio.* You command my house and secrecy.

*Isa.* I thank you, Violante. I wish you would oblige me with Mrs. Flora awhile.

*Vio.* [*Taps bell.*] I'll send her to you. I must watch if father be still asleep, or here will be no room for Felix.

[*Exit*, D. R. H. I E.

*Isa.* Well, I don't know what ails me ; methinks I wish I could find this stranger out. [*Goes* R. C.

*Re-enter* FLORA, L. U. E.

*Flora.* Does your ladyship want me, madam ?

*Isa.* Ay, Flora, I resolve to make you my confidant.

*Flora.* I shall endeavor to discharge my duty, madam.

*Isa.* I doubt it not, and desire you to accept this as a token of my gratitude.

*Flora.* O, I should have been your humble servant without a fee.

*Isa.* I believe it. But to the purpose—do you think, if you saw the gentleman who brought me hither, you should know him again ?

*Flora.* From a thousand, madam : I have an excellent memory where a handsome man is concerned. When he went away, he said he would return again immediately. I wonder he comes not.

*Isa.* Here, did you say ? You rejoice me—[*Crosses* L.] —though I'll not see him if he comes. Could not you contrive to give him a letter ?

*Flora.* With the air of a duenna.

*Isa.* Not in this house—you must veil and follow him. He must not know it comes from me.

*Flora.* What, do you take me for a novice in love affairs ? Though I have not practised the art since I have been in Donna Violante's service, yet I have not lost the theory of a chambermaid. [*Crosses up* L. *of table.* ISABELLA *sits.*] Do you write the letter, and leave the rest to me—here, here, here's pen, ink, and paper.

*Isa.* I'll do it in a minute. [*Sits at table,* C., *and writes.*

*Flora.* So! this is a business after my own heart : Love always takes care to reward his laborers. O, I long to see the other two moidores. Methinks there's a grace peculiar to the military in making a present.

*Isa.* [*Rises.*] So, I have done—now if he does but find this house again.

*Flora.* If he should not, I warrant, I'll find him, [*Crosses up* L.] if he's in Lisbon ; for I have a strong possession that he has two more moidores as good as ever were told.

[*Puts the letter into her bosom.*

*Re-enter* VIOLANTE, D. L. H. I E.

*Vio.* Flora, watch my papa ; he's fast asleep in his study : if you find him stir, give me notice. [FELIX *taps at the win-*

18

*dow*, L. H. 2 E.] Hark, I hear Felix at the window; admit him instantly, and then to your post.

[*Exit* FLORA, D. L. H. I E.

*Isa.* [*Crosses* R.] What say you, Violante? Is my brother come?

*Vio.* It is his signal at the window.

*Isa.* [*Kneels.*] O, Violante! I conjure thee by all the love thou bear'st to Felix, by thy own generous nature, nay more, by that unspotted virtue thou art mistress of, do not discover to my brother I am here!

*Vio.* Contrary to your desire, be assured I never shall. But where's the danger?

*Isa.* [*Rises.*] Art thou born in Lisbon, and ask that question? He'll think his honor blemished by my disobedience, and would restore me to my father, or kill me: therefore, dear, dear girl——

*Vio.* Depend upon my friendship; nothing shall draw the secret from these lips; not even Felix, though at the hazard of his love. I hear him coming; retire into that closet.

*Isa.* Remember, Violante, upon thy promise my very life depends. [*Exit* R. U. E.

*Vio.* When I betray thee, may I share thy fate!

*Enter* FELIX, D. L. U. E.

My Felix! [*Runs into his arms.*

*Fel.* [L. C.] My Violante! [*In a rapture.*

*Vio.* What hazards dost thou run for me? O, how shall I requite thee?

*Fel.* If, during this tedious, painful exile, thy thoughts have never wandered from thy Felix, thou hast made me more than satisfaction.

*Vio.* Can there be room within this heart for any but thyself? No, if the god of love were lost to all the rest of human kind, thy image would secure him in my breast: I am all truth, all love, all faith, and know no jealous fears.

*Fel.* My heart's the proper sphere where love resides: could he quit that, he would be nowhere found; and yet, Violante, I'm in doubt.

*Vio.* Did I ever give thee cause to doubt, my Felix?

*Fel.* True love has many fears, and fears as many eyes as fame; yet, sure, I think they see no fault in thee.  [COLONEL BRITON *taps at the window*, L. H. 2 E.]   What's that?

[*Taps again.*

*Vio.* What?   I hear nothing.                       [*Again.*

*Fel.* Ha!   What means this signal at your window?

*Vio.* Some one, perhaps, in passing by, might have accidentally hit it; it can be nothing else.

*Col. B.* [*Without, at window*, 2 E. L. H.]   Hist, hist! Donna Violante!   Donna Violante!

*Fel.* They use your name by accident, too, do they, madam?

[*Crosses to* R. H.

*Re-enter* FLORA, D. L. U. E.

*Flora.* [L. H., *aside to* VIOLANTE.]   There is a gentleman at the window, madam, which I fancy to be the same who brought Isabella hither.   Shall I admit him?

*Vio.* [C., *aside.*]   Admit distraction rather!   Thou art the cause of this, unthinking wretch!

*Fel.* [R. H.]   What, has Mrs. Scout brought you fresh intelligence?   Death, I'll know the bottom of this immediately.

[*About to go.*

*Flora.* Scout!   I scorn your words, seignior!   [*The* COLONEL *taps louder.  Aside.*]   It must be the Colonel—now to deliver my letter to him.                 *Exit* D. L. H. I E.

*Vio.* Nay, nay, nay, you must not leave me.

[*Runs and catches hold of him.*

*Fel.* O, 'tis not fair not to answer the gentleman, madam. It is none of his fault that his visit proves unseasonable.   Pray let me go : my presence is but a restraint upon you.   [*Struggles to get from her as the taps grow louder.*]   Hark, he grows impatient at your delay.   Why do you hold the man whose absence would oblige you?   Pray let me go, madam.   Consider the gentleman wants you at the window—— Confusion!

[*Struggles.*

*Vio.* It is not me he wants.

*Fel.* Death! not you? Is there another of your name in the house? [*Seizes her hand and leads her toward the window.*] But come on, convince me of the truth of what you say ; open the window. If his business does not lie with you, your conversation may be heard. This, and only this, can take off my suspicion. What, do you pause? [*Down stage,* R.] O, guilt! guilt! Have I caught you? Nay, then I'll leap the balcony. If I remember, this way also leads to it.      [*Goes.*

*Vio.* Hold, hold, hold, hold! not for the world you enter there! [*Aside.*] Which way shall I preserve his sister from his knowledge?

*Fel.* What, have I touched you? Do you fear your lover's life?

*Vio.* I fear for none but you. For goodness' sake, do not speak so loud, my Felix. If my father hears you, I am lost forever. [*With tenderness and reprovingly, one hand on his shoulder.*] Felix! Felix!—[*As he still looks angrily, her woman's pride gets the better of her love, and she goes toward the window.* FELIX *still holds her hand and follows her, listening as she throws open the window and speaks. She speaks slowly. As* BRITON *replies,* FELIX *starts a step, then turns and looks her in the face.*]—Your curiosity shall be satisfied. [*Goes to the window,* 2 E. L. H., *throws up the sash.*] Whoe'er you are, that with such insolence dare use my name, and give the neighborhood pretence to reflect upon my conduct, I charge you instantly to be gone, or expect the treatment you deserve.

*Col. B.* [*Without,* 2 E. L. H.] I ask pardon, madam, and will obey ; but, when I left this house to-night——

*Fel.* Good.

*Vio.* You are mistaken in the house, I suppose, sir.

*Fel.* No, no, he's not mistaken. Pray, madam, let the gentleman go on.

*Vio.* Pray be gone, sir ; I know of no business you have here.

*Col. B.* I wish I did not know it either. But this house contains my soul; then can you blame my body for hovering about it?

*Fel.* Beautiful! Beautiful!

*Vio.* I tell you again, you are mistaken; however, for your own satisfaction, call to-morrow.

*Fel.* Matchless impudence! an assignation before my face. [*Down* R., *crosses* L., *and up to window.*] No, he shall not live to meet your wishes.

[*Takes out a pistol, and goes toward window*, L. H. 2 E.; *she catches hold of him.*

*Vio.* Ah! [*Shrieks.*] Hold, I conjure you.

*Col. B.* To-morrow's an age, madam! May I not be admitted to-night?

*Vio.* If you be a gentleman, I command your absence. [*Aside.*] Unfortunate, what will my stars do with me?

*Col. B.* I have done. Only this—be careful of my life, for it is in your keeping.           [*Exit from the window.*

*Fel.* Pray observe the gentleman's request, madam.

[*Walks from her.*

*Vio.* I am all confusion.           [*Down* R.

*Fel.* You are all truth, all love, all faith; O, thou all women! How have I been deceived! 'Sdeath, could you not have imposed upon me for this one night? Could neither my faithful love, nor the hazard I have run to see you, make me worthy to be cheated on? O thou——

*Vio.* Felix!

*Fel.* [*Repeats.*] "When I left this house to-night." To-night—to-night!

*Vio.* [*Aside.*] O, Isabella! what hast thou involved me in?

*Fel.* [*Repeats.*] "This house contains my soul." O, sweet soul!

*Vio.* [*Aside.*] Yet I resolve to keep the secret.

*Fel.* [*Repeats.*] "Be careful of my life, for 'tis in your keeping." Fiends! Fiends! How ugly she appears!

[*Looks at her.*

*Vio.* Believe me, Felix, I have not injured you, nor am I false.

*Fel.* Not false? not injured me? O, Violante! Not false! O, monstrous!

*Vio.* Indeed, I am not. There is a cause, Felix—ah! which

I must not reveal. O, think how far honor can oblige your sex. Then allow a woman may be bound by the same rule to keep a secret.

*Fel.* Honor ! What hast thou to do with honor ? A secret ! ha, ha, ha ! his affairs are wondrous safe, who trusts his secrets to a woman's keeping ; but you need give yourself no trouble about clearing this point, madam, for you are become so indifferent to me, that your truth and falsehood are the same.

*Re-enter* FLORA, *door* L. H. I E.

*Flora.* So, I have delivered my letter to the Colonel, and received my fee.—Madam, your father bade me see what noise that was. [*Crosses* C.] For goodness' sake, sir, why do you speak so loud ?

*Fel.* Oh ! I understand my cue, mistress ; my absence is necessary, I'll oblige you.

[*Crosses* C. *Going.* VIOLANTE *takes hold of him.*

*Vio.* O, let me undeceive you first.

*Fel.* Impossible.

*Vio.* 'Tis very possible if I durst.

*Fel.* Durst ! ha, ha, ha ! durst !

*Vio.* Another time I'll tell thee all.

*Fel.* Nay, now or never.

*Vio.* Now it cannot be.

*Fel.* Then it shall never be. Most ungrateful of thy sex, farewell. [*Breaks from her, and exit,* D. L. H. I E.

*Vio.* Yet not even this shall draw the secret from me.

That I'll preserve, let fortune frown or smile :
And trust to love, my love to reconcile.


CURTAIN.

# ACT II.

SCENE I.—*A Handsome Chamber in Frederic's House.*

*Enter* LISSARDO *and* INIS, D. R. H. I E.

*Lis.* [C.] Your lady run away, and you know not whither, say you?

*Inis.* [R.] She never greatly cared for me after finding you and I together: but you are very grave, methinks, Lissardo.

*Lis.* [*Looking on the ring.*] Not at all. I have some thoughts, indeed, of altering my course of living; there is a critical minute in every man's life, which, if we can but lay hold of, he may make his fortune.

*Inis.* [*Aside.*] Ah! what do I see? a diamond ring? Where the deuce had he that ring?—You have got a very pretty ring there, Lissardo.

*Lis.* Ay, the trifle is pretty enough; but the lady which gave it to me is a beauty, I assure you.

[*Crosses* R. *Cocks his hat, and struts.*

*Inis.* I can't bear this—the lady. [*Aside.*] What lady, pray?

*Lis.* O fie! There's a question to ask à gentleman.

*Inis.* [C.] A gentleman! Is this your love for me? Ungrateful man, you'll break my heart, so you will.

[*Bursts into tears.*

*Lis.* [*Aside.*] Poor, tender-hearted fool.

*Inis.* If I knew who gave you that ring, I'd tear her eyes out, so I would. [*Sobs.*

*Lis.* [*Aside.*] So, now the jade wants a little coaxing. Why, what dost weep for now, my dear, ha?

*Inis.* I suppose Flora gave you that ring; but I'll——

[*Crosses* R.

*Lis.* No, the devil take me if she did ; you make me swear now—I did but joke ; the ring is none of mine, it is my master's ; I am to give it to be new set, that's all; therefore pr'ythee dry thy eyes, and kiss me, come.

*Enter* FLORA, *unobserved,* L. H. I E.

*Inis.* And do you really speak truth now ?

*Lis.* Why do you doubt it ?

*Flora.* [*Aside.*] So, so, very well ! I thought there was an intrigue between him and Inis, for all he has foresworn it so often. [*Goes up* L. C.

*Inis.* Nor ha'n't you seen Flora since you come to town ?

*Flora.* [*Aside* L.] Ha ! how dares she mention my name?

*Lis.* No, by this kiss, I ha'n't. [*Kisses her.*

*Flora.* [*Aside.*] Here's a dissembling varlet.

*Inis.* Nor don't you love her at all ?

*Lis.* Love the devil ! There, now you've made me swear again. Why, did I not always tell thee she was my aversion ?

*Flora.* Did you so, villain ? [*Gives him a box on the ear.*

*Lis.* [*Aside.*] Zounds, she's here ! I have made a fine piece of work on it. [*Crosses* L.

*Inis.* What's that for, ha ? [*Goes up to her.*

*Flora.* I shall tell you by and by, Mrs. Frippery, if you don't get about your business.

*Inis.* Who do you call Frippery, Mrs. Trollop ? Pray get about your business, if you go to that ; I hope you pretend to no right and title here. [*Crosses to* LISSARDO.

*Lis.* [*Aside.*] Do they take me for an acre of land, that they quarrel about right and title to me ?

*Flora.* Pray, what right have you, mistress, to ask that question ?

[LISSARDO, *up and down.* FLORA *and* INIS *separate.*

*Inis.* No matter for that ; I can show a better title to him than you, I believe.

*Lis.* Now my dears, don't exert yourselves so much about me : I might, in a modest way, satisfy both your demands upon me.

*Flora.* You satisfy! No, sirrah, I am not to be satisfied so soon as you think, perhaps.

*Inis.* No, nor I neither. What, do you make no difference between us?

*Flora.* You pitiful fellow, you! How often have you sworn to me that you hated Inis, and only carried fair for the good cheer she gave you; but that you could never like a woman with crooked legs, you said.

*Inis.* How, how crooked legs! [*Raises her dress a little.*

*Lis.* [*Drops down on his knee, and holds his hat before his eyes.*] Pr'ythee, my dear, moderate thy passion.

[*Coaxingly.*

*Inis.* I'd have you to know, sirrah, my legs were never——

*Flora.* [*Aside.*] I am glad I have done some mischief.

*Lis.* [*To* INIS.] Art thou really so foolish as to mind what an enraged woman says? Don't you see she does it on purpose to part you and I? [*Runs to* FLORA.] Could not you find the joke without putting yourself in a passion? you silly girl, you. Why, I saw you follow us plain enough, and said all this that you might not go back with only your labor for your pains. But come, kiss and be friends.

*Flora.* Don't think to coax me; hang your kisses.

[*The two maids go up and down,* LISSARDO *between them, and meet in* C., *as if to scratch at each other, when* FELIX'S *voice stops them.*

*Fel.* [*Without,* L. H. 1 E.] Lissardo!

*Lis.* [*Aside.*] Odsheart, here's my master; the devil take both these jades for me; what shall I do with them?

*Inis.* [*Aside.*] Ha! 'tis Don Felix's voice; I would not have him find me here with his footman for the world.

*Fel.* [*Without,* L. H.] Why, Lissardo, Lissardo!

*Lis.* Coming, sir. What a plague will you do?

*Flora.* Bless me, which way shall I get out?

*Lis.* [*Crosses* C.] Nay, nay, you must e'en set your quarrel aside, and be content to be mewed up in this clothes-press together, or stay where you are, and face it out—there is no help for it.

*Flora.* Put me anywhere, rather than that : come, come, let me in.

> [LISSARDO *opens door ; all three run up and jam in door-*
> *way,* INIS, *and* FLORA *face to face. Finally,* FLORA
> *exit, and* INIS *comes forward.*

*Inis.* I'll see her hanged before I'll go into the place where she is. I'll trust fortune for my deliverance. Here used to be a pair of back stairs ; I'll try to find them out.

> [*Exit* R. H. 2 E.]

*Enter* DON FELIX *and* FREDERIC, L. H. I E.

*Fel.* Was you asleep, sirrah, that you did not hear me call ?

*Lis.* I did hear you, and answered you I was coming, sir.

*Fel.* Go, get the horses ready ; I'll leave Lisbon to-night, never to see it more. [*Crosses.*

*Lis.* Hey-day! what's the matter now ? [*Exit* L. H. I E.

*Fred.* Pray tell me, Don Felix, what has ruffled your temper thus ?

*Fel.* [R.] A woman. O, friend, who can name woman, and forget inconstancy ?

*Fred.* Come, this is some groundless jealousy. Love raises many fears.

*Fel.* No, no ; my ears conveyed the truth into my heart, and reason justifies my anger. O, my friend! Violante's false, and I have nothing left but thee in Lisbon, which can make me wish ever to see it more ; except revenge upon my rival, of whom I am ignorant. O that some miracle would reveal him to me, that I might through his heart punish her infidelity!

*Enter* VASQUEZ, L. H. I E.

*Vas.* Sir, I bring you joyful news.

*Fel.* What's the matter ?

*Vas.* I am told that Don Antonio is out of danger, and now in the palace.

*Fel.* I wish it be true ; then I'm at liberty to watch my rival, and pursue my sister. Pr'ythee, Frederic, inform thyself of the truth of this report. [*Paces up and down.*

*Fred.* [*Crosses.*] I will this minute. Do you hear ?—[*To* VASQUEZ.] Let nobody in to Don Felix till my return.

[*Exit* L. H. I E.

*Vas.* I'll observe, sir. [*Exit* L. H. I E.

*Flora.* [*Opens door*, R. F.] They have almost frightened me out of my wits, I'm sure. Now Felix is alone, I have a good mind to pretend I came with a message from my lady; but how then shall I say I came into the cupboard ?

*Vas.* [*Without*, L. H. I E.] I tell you, madam, Don Felix is not here.

*Vio.* [*Without*, L. H. I E.] I tell you, sir, he is here, and I will see him.

*Fel.* What noise is that ?


*Enter* VIOLANTE, L. H. D.


*Flora.* My stars ! My lady here ! [*Closes door.*

*Vio.* You are as difficult of access, sir, as a first minister of state.

[*Unveils, courtesies very ceremoniously, and smiles at his surly looks.*

*Fel.* If your visit was destined to Frederic, madam, he is abroad.

*Vio.* No, sir, the visit is to you.

*Fel.* You are very punctual in your ceremonies, madam.

*Vio.* Though I did not come to return your visit, but to take that which your civility ought to have brought me.

*Fel.* If my eyes, my ears, and my understanding lied, then I am in your debt; else not, madam.

[*She is surprised and offended at his saying so gross a word.*

*Vio.* I will not charge them with a term so gross, to say they lied, but call it a mistake [*Crosses* C.] ; nay, call it anything to excuse my Felix. Could I, think ye, could I put off my pride so far, poorly to dissemble a passion which I did not feel, or seek a reconciliation with what I did not love? No law, whilst single, binds us to obey ; but your sex are obliged to pay a deference to all womankind.

*Fel.* These are fruitless arguments. 'Tis most certain thou wert dearer to these eyes than all that heaven e'er gave to charm the sense of man; but I would rather tear them out, than suffer them to delude my reason, and enslave my peace.

*Vio.* Can you love without esteem? and where is the esteem for her you still suspect? O, Felix, there is a delicacy in love, which equals even a religious faith! True love never doubts the object it adores, and sceptics there will disbelieve their sight.

*Fel.* Your notions are too refined for mine, madam.

*Re-enter* VASQUEZ, L. H. I E.

How now, sirrah, what do you want?

*Vas.* Only my master's cloak out of this press, sir; that's all.       [*Crosses behind to* D. R. F.

*Fel.* Make haste then.

*Vas.* [*Opens the door*, R. F., *and sees* FLORA.] O, the devil! the devil!       [*Exit* L. H. I E.

*Flora.* Discovered! Nay, then, legs befriend me.
      [*Crosses stage and runs out*, L. H. I E.

*Vio.* A woman concealed! Very well, Felix!

*Fel.* A woman in the press!

*Re-enter* LISSARDO, L. H. I E.

*Lis.* Sir, the horses are——

*Fel.* How the devil came a woman there, sirrah?
      [*Seizes* LISSARDO, *and throws him round*.

*Lis.* [*Aside.*] What shall I say now?

*Vio.* Now, Lissardo, show your wit, to bring your master off.

*Lis.* Off, madam? Nay, nay, nay, there, there needs no great wit to, to, to, bring him off, madam; for she did, and she did not come, as, as, as a, a, a man may say, directly to, to, to, to speak with my master, madam.

*Vio.* I see by your stammering, Lissardo, that your invention is at a very low ebb.

*Fel.* 'Sdeath, rascal! speak without hesitation, and the truth too, or I shall run you through and through.

*Vio.* No, no, your master mistakes; he would not have you speak the truth.

*Fel.* Madam, my sincerity wants no excuse.

*Lis.* [*Aside.*] I am so confounded between one and the other, that I can't think of a lie.

*Fel.* Sirrah, fetch me this woman back instantly; I'll know what business she had here!

*Vio.* Not a step; your master shall not be put to the blush. [LISSARDO *bows as if to say: "You see, sir, I can't help it," and goes up.*] Come, a truce, Felix! Do you ask me no more questions about the window, and I'll forgive this.

*Fel.* I scorn forgiveness where I own no crime; but your soul, conscious of its guilt, would fain lay hold of this occasion to blend your treason with my innocence.

*Vio.* Insolent! Nay, if instead of owning your fault, you endeavor to insult my patience, I must tell you, sir, you don't behave yourself like that man of honor you would be taken for; you ground your quarrel with me upon inconstancy; 'tis plain you are false yourself, and would make me the aggressor. It was not for nothing the fellow opposed my entrance. This last usage has given me back my liberty, [*Crosses to* L. H.] and now my father's will shall be obeyed without the least reluctance: [*With stern formality, and throwing her veil over her face, as she exits.*] and so your servant.

[*Exit* L. H. I E.

*Fel.* O, [*Goes* R.] stubborn, stubborn heart, what wilt thou do? Her father's will shall be obeyed; ha! that carries her to a cloister, and cuts off all my hopes at once. By Heaven, she shall not, must not leave me! No, she is not false; at least my love now represents her true, because I fear to lose her. Ha! villain, art thou here? [*Turns upon* LISSARDO, *who is trying to steal off*, L. U. E.] Tell me this moment who this woman was, and for what intent she was here concealed— or—— [*Drawing his sword.*

*Lis.* Ay, good sir, forgive me, and I'll tell you the whole truth. [*Falls on his knees.*

*Fel.* Out with it then.

[*Threatening with his sword quite at* LISSARDO'S *mouth.*

*Lis.* It, it, it was——

*Fel.* Who? Who?

*Lis.* Mrs. Flora, sir, Donna Violante's woman. You must know, sir, we have had——

*Fel.* What? What?

*Lis.* A sneaking kindness for one another a great while. She was not willing you should know it; so, when she heard your voice, she ran into the clothes-press. I would have told you this at first, but I was afraid of her lady's knowing it; this is the truth, as I hope for a whole skin, sir.

*Fel.* If it be not, I'll not leave you a whole bone in it, sirrah. Fly, and observe if Violante goes directly home.

*Lis.* Yes, sir, yes.

*Fel.* Fly, you dog, fly. [*Exit* LISSARDO, L. H. I E.] I must convince her of my faith. O, how irresolute is a lover's heart! How absolute is a woman's power!

In vain we strive their tyranny to quit;
In vain we struggle, for we must submit.

[*Exit* D. R. H. I E.

CURTAIN.

# ACT III.

## Scene i.— *The Street.*

*Enter* GIBBY, L.

*Gibby.* Ay, this is bony wark indeed ! to run three hundred mile to this wicked town, and before I can well fill my weam, to be sent a hunting after this black she-devil ! What gate sal I gang to speer for this wutch now ! Ah, for a ruling elder, or the kirk's treasurer, or his mon, I'd gar my master mak twa o'this. But I am sure there's na sic honest people here, or there wud na be sa mickle sculddudrie.

*Enter* VIOLANTE, 1 E. R. H.

I vow, madam, but I am glad that ye and I are foregathered.

*Vio.* What would the fellow have ?

*Gibby.* Nothing away, madam, no worth yer heart, what a muckle deal o' mischief had you like to bring upon poor Gibby.

*Vio.* The man's drunk.

*Gibby.* In troth am I not. And gin I had no found ye, madam, the Laird knows when I should ; for my master bad me ne'er gang hame without tidings of ye, madam.

*Vio.* Sirrah, get about your business, or I'll have your bones drubbed.                                   [*Crosses* L. H.

*Gibby.* Geud faith, my maister has e'en done that t'yer honds, madam.

*Vio.* Who is your master, sir ?

*Gibby.* It is no sa lang sen ye parted wi' him. I wish he ken ye hafe as weel as ye ken him.

32

*Vio.* Poh, the creature's mad, or mistakes me for somebody else ; and I should be as mad as he, to talk to him any longer.

[*Exit into* DON PEDRO'S *house*, D. F. L. H.

*Enter* LISSARDO, R. H. I E. *Crosses* L.

*Lis.* So, she's gone home, I see. What did that Scotch fellow want with her ? I'll try to find it out ; perhaps I may discover something that may make my master friends with me again.

*Gibby.* [R.] Are ye gone, madam ? A deel scope in yer company ; for I'm as weese as I was. But I'll bide and see wha's house it is, gin I can meet with ony civil body to speer at. [*Turns and sees* LISSARDO. *Crosses* L.] My lad, wot ye wha lives in your hoose ?

*Lis.* Don Pedro de Mendoza.

*Gibby.* And did you see a lady gang in but now ?

*Lis.* Yes, I did.

*Gibby.* And d'ye ken her tee ?

*Lis.* It was Donna Violante, his daughter. [*Aside.*] What the devil makes him so inquisitive ! There is something in it, that's certain. 'Tis a cold morning, brother ; what think you of a dram ?

*Gibby.* In troth, very well, sir.

*Lis.* You seem an honest fellow ; pr'ythee, let's drink to our better acquaintance. [*Both going* R.

*Gibby.* Wi' aw my heart, sir ; gang your gate to the next house, and I'se follow ye.

*Lis.* Come along, then. [*Exit* R. H. I E.

*Gibby.* Don Pedro de Mendoza — Donna Violante, his daughter. That's as right as my leg, now ; I'se need na mare ; I'll tak a drink, and then to my maister. [*Exit* R. H. I E.

33

SCENE 2.—DONNA VIOLANTE'S *Apartments. Same as in Second Act.*

*Enter* ISABELLA, *in a gay temper,* L. U. E., *and* VIOLANTE, *out of humor,* R. U. E.

*Isa.* My dear, I have been seeking you this half hour, to tell you the most lucky adventure.

*Vio.* And you have pitched upon the most unlucky hour for it that you could possibly have found in the whole four and twenty.

*Isa.* I have seen the man I like.

*Vio.* And I have seen the man that I could wish to hate.

[*Rises, crosses* H.

*Isa.* And you must assist me in discovering whether he can like me or not.

*Vio.* You have assisted me in such a discovery already, I thank ye.

*Isa.* What say you, my dear?

*Vio.* I say I am very unlucky at discoveries, Isabella; I have too lately made one pernicious to my ease. Your brother is false.

*Isa.* Impossible!

*Vio.* Most true.

*Isa.* Some villain has traduced him to you.

*Vio.* No, Isabella; I love too well to trust the eyes of others; I never credit the ill-judging world, or form suspicions upon vulgar censures. No; I had ocular proof of his ingratitude. But tell me, Isabella, how can I serve you?

*Isa.* Thus, then: the gentleman that brought me hither I have seen and talked with upon the Terriero de Passa this morning, and I find him a man of sense, generosity, and good humor; in short, he is everything that I could like for a husband; and I have despatched Mrs. Flora to bring him hither; I hope you'll forgive the liberty I have taken.

*Vio.* Hither! to what purpose?

*Isa.* To the great universal purpose—matrimony.

[*Crosses* L.

34

*Vio.* Matrimony !  Why, do you design to ask him ?

*Isa.* No, Violante ; you must do that for me.

*Vio.* I thank you for the favor you design me, but desire to be excused. I manage my own affairs too ill to be trusted with those of other people. I can't, for my life, admire your conduct—to encourage a person altogether unknown to you. 'Twas very imprudent to meet him this morning, but much more so to send for him hither, knowing what inconveniency you have already drawn upon me.

*Isa.* I am not insensible how far my misfortunes have embarrassed you. Then do not deny me this last request, when a few hours, perhaps, may render my condition able to clear thy fame, and bring my brother to thy feet for pardon.

*Vio.* I suppose he knows you are the same woman that he brought in here last night ?

*Isa.* Not a syllable of that. I met him veiled ; and to prevent his knowing the house, I ordered Mrs. Flora to bring him by the back door into the garden.

*Vio.* The very way which Felix comes ; if they should meet there would be fine work. Indeed, my dear, I can't approve of your design.

*Enter* FLORA, D. L. H. I E.

*Flora.* [C.]   Madam, the Colonel waits your pleasure.

*Vio.* How durst you go upon such a message, mistress, without acquainting me.

*Flora.* So I am huffed for everything.

*Isa.* 'Tis too late to dispute that now, dear Violante ; I acknowledge the rashness of the action, but consider the necessity of my deliverance.

*Vio.* That indeed is a weighty consideration. Well, what am I to do ?

*Isa.* In the next room I'll give you instructions. In the mean time, Mrs. Flora, show the Colonel into this.

[*Exeunt* FLORA, D. L. H. I E., ISABELLA *and* VIOLANTE, D. R. H. I E.

FLORA *opens door and beckons to* COLONEL BRITON, *who enters.*

*Flora.* The lady will wait on you presently, sir.
[*Exit* D. L. H. I E.

*Col. B.* Very well.  This is a very fruitful soil; I have not been here quite four and twenty hours, and I have three affairs upon my hands already.

*Re-enter* VIOLANTE, D. R. U. E., *veiled.*

[*Aside.*] Ha! a fine-sized woman.  Pray Heaven she proves handsome.  I am come to obey your ladyship's commands.

*Vio.* Are you sure of that, Colonel?

*Col. B.* If you be not very unreasonable indeed, madam.  A man is but a man.                [*Takes her hand and kisses it.*

*Vio.* Nay, we have no time for compliments, Colonel. [*Crosses* L.]  Did you never see a woman in all your travels that you could like for a wife?

*Col. B.* [*Aside.*]  A very odd question.  Do you really expect that I should speak truth now?

*Vio.* I do, if you expect to be dealt with, Colonel.

*Col. B.* Why, then, yes.

*Vio.* Is she in your country, or this?

*Col. B.* [*Aside.*]  This is a very pretty kind of a catechism.—In this town, I believe, madam.

*Vio.* Her name is——

*Col. B.* Ay, how is she called, madam?

*Vio.* Nay, I ask you that, sir.

*Col. B.* O, O! why, she is called—— Pray, madam, how is it you spell your name?

*Vio.* O, Colonel, I am not the happy woman, nor do I wish it.                [*Crosses* R.

*Col. B.* No?  I am sorry for that.  [*Aside.*]  What the devil does she mean by all these questions?

*Vio.* Come, Colonel, for once be sincere; perhaps you may not repent it.

*Col. B.* Faith, madam, I have an inclination to sincerity ; but I'm afraid you'll call my manners in question.

*Vio.* Not at all ; I prefer truth before compliment in this affair.

*Col. B.* Why, then, to be plain with you, madam, a lady last night wounded my heart by a fall from a window, whose person I could be content to take, as my father took my mother, till death do us part ; but who she is, or how distinguished, whether maid, wife, or widow, I can't inform you. Perhaps you are she.

*Vio.* Not to keep you in suspense, I am not she, [*Crosses* L.] but I can give you an account of her. That lady is a maid of condition, has ten thousand pounds ; and if you are a single man, her person and fortune are at your service.

*Col. B.* I accept the offer with the highest transports ; but say, my charming angel, art thou not she ?

[*Offers to embrace her.*

*Vio.* Once again, Colonel, I tell you I am not she ; but at six this evening you shall find her on the Terriero de Passa, with a white handkerchief in her hand. Get a priest ready, and you know the rest.

*Col. B.* I shall infallibly observe your directions, madam.

*Re-enter* FLORA, D. L. H. I E., *hastily, and whispers* VIOLANTE, *who starts and seems surprised.*

*Vio.* Ha ! Felix crossing the garden, say you ? What shall I do now?

*Col. B.* You seem surprised, madam.

*Vio.* O Colonel, my father is coming hither ; and if he finds you here I am ruined.

*Col. B.* Odslife, madam, thrust me anywhere. Can't I go out this way ? [*Crosses up* L.

*Vio.* No, no, no—he comes that way. How shall I prevent their meeting ? [*Hesitates—advances a step—again stops in suspense, then resolutely.*] Here, here, step into my bed-chamber—— And be still, as you value her you love. Don't stir till you've notice, as ever you hope to have her.

*Col. B.* On that condition I'll not breathe. [*Exit* D. R. H. I E.

[VIOLANTE *places chair and sits in centre, picks up a book, and pretends to be absorbed in it.* FLORA *sits and pretends to sleep, her head and arms on table. When* FELIX *addresses* VIOLANTE, *she rouses* FLORA *with some difficulty.*

*Enter* FELIX, D. L. H. I E.

*Fel.* I wonder where this dog of a servant is all this while. But she is at home, I find. [*Aside.*] How coldly she regards me.—You look, Violante, as if the sight of me were troublesome to you.

*Vio.* Can I do otherwise, when you have the assurance to approach me after what I saw to-day?

*Fel.* Assurance ! rather call it good-nature, after what I heard last night. Pray give me leave to ask your woman one question ; my man assures me she was the person you saw at my lodgings.

*Flora.* [L.] I confess it, madam, and ask your pardon.

*Vio.* Impudent baggage, not to undeceive me sooner! What business could you have there ?

*Fel.* Lissardo and she, it seems, imitate you and me.

[*She rises.*

*Flora.* I love to follow the example of my betters, madam.

*Fel.* I hope I am justified——

*Vio.* [*Crosses* R.] Since we are to part, Felix, there needs no justification.

*Fel.* Methinks you talk of parting as a thing indifferent to you. Can you forget how I have loved ?

*Vio.* I wish I could forget my own passion ; I should with less concern remember yours. But for Mrs. Flora——

*Fel.* You must forgive her. Must, did I say ? I fear I have no power to impose, though the injury was done to me.

[*Crosses* R.

*Vio.* 'Tis harder to pardon an injury done to what we love than to ourselves ; but at your request, Felix, I do forgive

38

her. Go watch my father, Flora, lest he should awake and surprise us.

*Flora.* Yes, madam.                  [*Exit*, D. L. U. E.

*Fel.* Dost thou, then, love me, Violante ?

*Vio.* What need of repetition from my tongue, when every look confesses what you ask ?

*Fel.* O, let no man judge of love but those who feel it ! What wondrous magic lies in one kind look ! One tender word destroys a lover's rage, and melts his fiercest passion into soft complaint. O, the window, Violante ; wouldst thou but clear that one suspicion !

*Vio.* Pr'ythee no more of that, my Felix ; a little time shall bring thee perfect satisfaction.

*Re-enter* FLORA, D. L. H. I E., *hastily.*

*Flora.* [L.] O, madam, madam, madam, my lord, your father, has been in the house, and locked the back door, and comes muttering to himself this way.

*Vio.* [C.] Then we are caught. Now, Felix, we are undone.

*Fel.* [R.] Heaven forbid ! This is most unlucky ! Let me step into your chamber ; there I may conceal myself.

[*Runs to the door*, R. H. I E., *and puts his hand on the door-knob.* VIOLANTE *follows him, and draws him away, step by step. He keeps his eyes on the door. Pause.*

*Vio.* No, no, Felix, that's no safe place ; my father often goes thither, and should you cough or sneeze, we are lost.

*Fel.* [*Aside.*] Either my eye deceived me, or I saw a man within. I'll watch him close.

*Flora.* O, invention, invention ! I have it, madam. Here, here, sir ; off with your sword and hat, and I'll fetch you a disguise.            [*Puts* FELIX'S *hat on table.*

*Fel.* [*Aside.*] She shall deal with the devil if she conveys him out without my knowledge.

*Vio.* Bless me, how I tremble !

*Re-enter* FLORA, D. F. R. H., *with a disguise dress—a riding-hood and skirt—old woman's dress. Both assist him to disguise.* FELIX *tries to get into front of gown, like pantaloons.*

*Flora.* [R.] Here, sir, put on this.
*Flora.* [*Before this.*] Now give me your hat. [*He does so.*] Now your gloves. [*He does so.*] Now your sword.
*Felix.* [*His eyes on door.*] No—not my sword.
*Flora.* Be sure you don't speak a word.
*Fel.* [R.] Not for the Indies.                    [*Puts on dress.*
*Ped.* [*Without,* L. H. I E.] Why, how came the garden door open ?

*Enter* DON PEDRO, L. H. I E.

Ha! how now ? Whom have we here ?
*Flora.* [R. C.] 'Tis my mother, and please you, sir. [FELIX *and* FLORA *courtesy.*]
*Ped.* [C.] Your mother! By St. Andrew, she's a strapper! Why, you are a dwarf to her. How many children have you, good woman ?
*Vio.* [L., *aside.*] O, if he speaks we are lost !
*Flora.* O dear, seignior, she cannot hear you ; she has been deaf these twenty years.
*Ped.* Alas, poor woman! Why, you muffle her up as if she was blind, too ; turn up her hood.
*Vio.* [*Aside.*] Undone forever ! St. Anthony forbid !—O, sir, she has the dreadfulest unlucky eyes ! Pray don't look upon them ; I made her keep her hood shut on purpose. O, O, O, O !
*Ped.* Eyes ! Why, what's the matter with her eyes !
*Flora.* My poor mother, sir, is much afflicted with the colic.
*Pedro.* What ! Has she got colic in her eyes ?
*Flora.* About two months ago she had it grievously in her stomach, and was over-persuaded to take a dram of filthy English Geneva, which immediately flew up into her head, and caused such a defluction in her eyes that she could never since bear the daylight.

*Ped.* Say you so? Poor woman! Well, make her sit down, Violante, and give her a glass of wine.

*Vio.* Let her daughter give her a glass below, sir. For my part, she has frightened me so, I sha'n't be myself these two hours. I am sure her eyes are evil eyes.

*Ped.* [R.] Well, well, do so. Evil eyes! there are no evil eyes, child.

*Flora.* [*Speaks loud.*] Come along, mother.

[*Crossing* L. U. E.

*Ped.* Good-by. Take care how you go down, good woman.

[FELIX *stops to courtesy three times, and stumbles over the threshold of the door.* FLORA *re-enters almost immediately, and gets* FELIX'S *hat and gloves, concealing them behind her coat again;* VIOLANTE *engaging her father's attention.*

[*Exeunt* FELIX *and* FLORA, D. L. H. I E.

*Vio.* [*Aside.*] I'm glad he's gone.

*Ped.* Hast thou heard the news, Violante?

*Vio.* What news, sir?

*Ped.* Why, Vasquez tells me that Don Lopez's daughter, Isabella, is run away from her father. Oh, he has very ill fortune with his children. [*Aside.*] Well, I'm glad my daughter has no inclination to matrimony, that my house is plagued with no suitors.

*Vio.* This is the first word I ever heard of it; I pity her frailty!

*Ped.* Well said, Violante. Next week I intend thy happiness shall begin.

*Vio.* [*Aside.*] I don't intend to stay so long, thank you, papa.

*Ped.* My lady abbess writes word she longs to see thee, and has provided everything in order for thy reception.


*Re-enter* FLORA, D. L. H. I E.


Thou wilt lead a happy life, my girl—fifty times before that of matrimony, where an extravagant coxcomb might make a beggar of thee, or an ill-natured, surly dog break thy heart.

*Flora.* [L., *aside.*] Break her heart! She had as good have her bones broke as to be a nun; I am sure I had rather, of the two. You are wondrous kind, sir; but if I had such a father, I know what I would do.

*Ped.* Why, what would you do, minx—ha?

*Flora.* [*Crosses to him.*] I would tell him I had as good a right and title.

*Ped.* You would, mistress! Who the devil doubts it? You are enough to spoil your lady, housewife, if she had not abundance of devotion.

*Vio.* Fie, Flora; are you not ashamed to talk thus to my father? You said, yesterday, you would be glad to go with me into the monastery.

*Flora.* Did I? I told a great lie, then.

*Ped.* She go with thee! No, no; she's enough to corrupt the whole convent. Well, child, remember what I said to thee: next week I am going into the country for two or three days, to settle some affairs with thy uncle; and when I return, we'll provide for thy happiness, child. Good-by, Violante; take care of thyself.

[*Exeunt* DON PEDRO *and* VIOLANTE, D. L. H. 1 E.

*Flora.* [*Watches them off.*] So, now for the Colonel. Hist, hist, Colonel.

### Re-enter COLONEL BRITON, D. R. H. 1 E.

*Col. B.* Is the coast clear?

*Flora.* Yes, if you can climb; for you must get over the wash-house, and jump from the garden wall into the street.

*Col. B.* Nay, nay, I don't value my neck, if my incognita answers but thy lady's promise.

[*Exeunt* COLONEL BRITON *and* FLORA, D. F. R. H.

### Re-enter FELIX, D. L. H. 1 E.

*Fel.* I have lain perdue under the stairs, till I watched the old man out. [VIOLANTE *opens the door*, L. H. 1 E.] 'Sdeath, I am prevented. [*Goes up to observe.*

*Re-enter* VIOLANTE, D. L. H. I E.

*Vio.* Now to set my prisoner at liberty. [*She takes four steps stealthily, starts, turns and looks* L. FELIX, *watching her, advances to* R. *Pause.* VIOLANTE *then goes to door where the* COLONEL *was hid.*] Sir, sir, you may appear.

FELIX, *who has been following her up to the door, seizes her and turns her over to* L.

*Fel.* Treacherous woman !
*Vio.* [*Aside.*] Felix here ! Then all's discovered.
*Fel.* [*Draws.* Turns VIOLANTE *to* L. H.] Villain, whoever thou art, come out, I charge thee, and take the reward of thy villainous errand.
*Vio.* [*Aside.*] What shall I say ? Nothing but the secret which I have sworn to keep can reconcile this quarrel.
*Fel.* A coward ! Nay, then, I'll fetch you out. Think not to hide thyself ; no, by St. Anthony, an altar should not protect thee. [*Exit* R. H. D. I E.
*Vio.* [*Aside.*] Defend me, Heaven ! What shall I do ? I must discover Isabella, or here will be murder.
[*Sinks into chair, overpowered.*

*Re-enter* FLORA, *quickly, with a gliding step, throwing her hands up in joy.*

*Flora.* I have helped the Colonel off clear, madam.
[*Exit with a quick side step.*
*Vio.* Say'st thou so, my girl ? Then I am armed.
[*Sits* C., *with her eyes riveted on* FELIX, *and laughing at him, as he re-enters* R. I E. VIOLANTE *bursts into a loud fit of laughter, and points at him in derision, as he rushes on with his back to audience. Pause. He turns from her in amazement, then turns to her again.*
*Fel.* Where has the devil, in compliance to your sex, conveyed him from my resentment ?

43

*Vio.* Him! whom do you mean, my dear, inquisitive spark? Ha, ha, ha! Will you never leave these jealous whims?

*Fel.* Will you never cease to impose upon me?

*Vio.* You impose upon yourself, my dear. Do you think I did not see you? Yes, I did, and resolved to put this trick upon you.         [*Imitates her manner of crossing* R.

*Fel.* Trick! Trick! Trick!

*Vio.* Yes, trick. I knew you'd take the hint, and soon relapse into your wonted error. How easily your jealousy is fired! I shall have a blessed life with you.

*Fel.* Was there nothing in it, then, but only to try me?

*Vio.* Won't you believe your eyes?

*Fel.* My eyes! no, nor my ears, nor any of my senses, for they have all deceived me. [*Crosses to* R.] The moment a man lets a woman know her conquest, he resigns his senses, and sees nothing but what she'd have him.

*Vio.* And as soon as a woman finds her love returned, she becomes as errant a slave as if she had already said yes, at the altar.

*Fel.* The priest, Violante, would dissipate those fears which cause these quarrels. When wilt thou make me happy?

*Vio.* To-morrow I will tell thee. [*Crosses* R., *they meet*, C.] But, leave me now, lest some accident should bring my father.

*Fel.* To-morrow, then——
Fly swift, ye hours, and bring to-morrow on—
                        [*Kisses her hand.*

*Vio.* To-morrow. We shall meet to part no more.

*Fel.* O, rapt'rous sounds!
Do thou, like me, each doubt and fear remove.
And all to come be confidence and love.

        [*Exeunt* FELIX, D. L. U. E., VIOLANTE, D. R. H. I E.

CURTAIN.

# ACT IV.

*Enter* FELIX *and* FREDERIC R. H. I E.

*Fel.* This hour has been propitious ! I am reconciled to Violante, and you assure me Antonio is out of danger.

*Fred.* Your satisfaction is doubly mine.

*Enter* LISSARDO, L.

*Fel.* What haste you made, sirrah, to bring me word if Violante went home !

*Lis.* I can give you very good reasons for my stay, sir.— Yes, sir, she went home.

*Fred.* O, your master knows that, for he has been there himself, Lissardo.

*Lis.* Sir, may I beg the favor of your ear ?

*Fel.* What have you to say ?

[LISSARDO *whispers, and* FELIX *seems uneasy.*

*Fred.* Ha ! Felix changes color at Lissardo's news. What can it be ?

*Fel.* A Scotch footman, that belongs to Colonel Briton, an acquaintance of Frederic's, say you ? The devil !—— [*Aside.*] If she be false, by Heaven I'll trace her. [*Whispers* LISSARDO *and sends him off,* L. H. I E.] Pr'ythee, Frederic, do you know one Colonel Briton, a Scotchman ?

*Fred.* Yes. Why do you ask me ?

*Fel.* Nay, no great matter ; but my man tells me that he has had some little differences with a servant of his ; that's all.

*Fred.* He is a good, harmless, innocent fellow ; I am sorry for it. The Colonel lodges in my house. I knew him formerly

45

in England, and met him here by accident last night, and gave him an invitation home. He is a gentleman of good estate, besides his commission ; of excellent principles and strict honor, I assure you. [*Crosses* L.] Here he comes.

*Enter* COLONEL BRITON, L. H. I E.

Colonel, I began to think I had lost you.

*Col. B.* And not without some reason, if you knew all.

*Fel.* There's no danger of a fine gentleman's being lost in this town, sir.

*Col. B.* [*Crosses* C.] That compliment don't belong to me, sir—but I assure you I have been very near being run away with.

*Fred.* Who attempted it ?

*Col. B.* Faith, I know not—only that she is a charming woman—I mean as much as I saw of her.

*Fel.* [*Aside.*] My heart swells with apprehension. Some accidental rencounter ?

*Fred.* Come, unfold.

[*The* COLONEL *takes an arm of each and draws them close to him, telling his story with great gusto*—FELIX, *in an agony of suppressed irritation.*

*Col. B.* Why, then, you must know, gentlemen, that I was conveyed to her lodgings, by one of Cupid's emissaries, called a chambermaid, in a chair, through fifty blind alleys, who, by the help of a key, let me into a garden.

*Fel.* [*Aside.*] 'Sdeath, a garden ! This must be Violante's garden.

*Col. B.* From thence conducted me into a spacious room, told me her lady would wait on me presently ; so, without unveiling, modestly withdrew.

*Fel.* [*Aside.*] Damn her modesty ! This was Flora !

*Fred.* Well, how then, Colonel ?

*Col. B.* Then, sir, immediately from another door issued forth a lady, armed at both eyes, from whence such showers of darts fell around me that, had I not been covered with the shield of another beauty, I had infallibly fallen a martyr to her charms; for, you must know, I just saw her eyes—eyes, did I say? No, no, hold, I saw but one eye, though I suppose it had a fellow equally as killing.

*Fel.* Well, well, sir, what then?

[*Pretending to laugh, but his face, turned aside, showing intense ill-humor.*

*Col. B.* Why, upon her maid's giving notice her father was coming, she thrust me into the bed-chamber.

*Fel.* Upon her father's coming?

*Col. B.* Ay, so she said; but, putting my ear to the keyhole of the door, I found it was another lover.

*Fel.* [*Aside.*] Confound the jilt! 'Twas she, without dispute.

[*Up and down the stage.*

*Fred.* Ah, poor Colonel! Ha, ha, ha!

*Col. B.* I discovered they had had a quarrel; but whether they were reconciled or not, I can't tell; for the second alarm brought the father in good earnest, and had like to have made the gentleman and me acquainted; but she found some other stratagem to convey him out.

*Fel.* Contagion seize her, and make her body as ugly as her soul! There is nothing left to doubt of now. 'Tis plain 'twas she. [FREDERIC *and* COLONEL *laugh. Aside.*] Sure he knows me, and takes this method to insult me. 'Sdeath, I cannot bear it!

*Col. B.* [*To* FELIX—*playfully taking his arm and turning him around.* FELIX *turns away.* COLONEL *pulls him around again.*] Why, you don't seem to enjoy the joke.

*Fel.* Oh, yes, I do. Ha, ha, ha!

[*Tries to join in laugh, but ends with a groan.*

*Col. B.* But, sir, dear sir, do hearken to this. The nymph that introduced me, conveyed me out again over the top of a high wall, where I ran the danger of having my neck broke, for the father, it seems, had locked the door by which I entered.

*Fel.* [*Aside.*] That way I missed him. Damn her invention. Pray, Colonel—— [COLONEL *and* FELIX *laugh.*] Ha, ha, ha! it's very pleasant. Ha, ha!—was this the same lady you met upon the Terriero de Passa, this morning?

*Col. B.* Faith, I can't tell, sir ; I had a design to know who that lady was, but my dog of a footman, whom I had ordered to watch her home, fell fast asleep. I gave him a good beating for his neglect, and I have never seen the rascal since.

*Fred.* Here he comes. [FELIX *pacing the stage to and fro.*

*Enter* GIBBY, L. H. I E.

*Col. B.* Where have you been, sirrah ?

*Gibby.* Truth, I'se been seeking ye, and lik yer honor, these twa hoors and mair. I bring thee glad teedings, sir.

*Col. B.* What, have you found the lady ?

*Gibby.* [*Crosses* C.] Geud faith, ha' I, sir; and she's called Donna Violante, and her parent Don Pedro de Mendosa ; and, gin ye will gang wi' me, and lik yer honor, I'se make ye ken the hoose right weel.

*Fel.* [*Aside.*] O, torture, torture !                    [*Up stage.*

*Col. B.* [*Aside.*] Ha ! Violante ! That's the lady's name of the house where my incognita is : sure it could not be her ; at least it was not the same house, I am confident.

*Fred.* Violante ! 'Tis false; I would not have you credit him, Colonel.

*Gibby.* The deel tak me, sir, gin I lee.

*Fel.* Sirrah, I say you do lie, and I'll make you eat it, you dog; [*Seizing him and throwing him over—kicks him.*] and if your master will justify you——

*Col. B.* Not I, faith, sir. I answer for nobody's lies but my own. If you please, kick him again.

*Gibby.* [*Gets* R.] But gin he does, I'se na tak it, sir, gin he was a thousand Spaniards.          [*Walks about in a passion.*

*Col. B.* I owed you a beating, sirrah, and I am obliged to this gentleman for taking the trouble off my hands ; therefore say no more ; d'ye hear, sir.          [*Apart to* GIBBY.

*Gibby.* Troth de I, sir, and feel tee.

*Fred.* This must be a mistake, Colonel; for I know Violante perfectly well, and I am certain she would not meet you upon the Terriero de Passa.

*Col. B.* Don't be too positive, Frederic. Now I have some reasons to believe it was that very lady.

*Fel.* You'll very much oblige me, sir, if you'd let me know these reasons.

*Col. B.* Sir!

*Fel.* [C.] Sir, I say I have a right to inquire into these reasons you speak of.

*Col. B.* [L. C.] Ha, ha! really, sir, I cannot conceive how you, or any man, can have a right to inquire into my thoughts.

*Fel.* Sir, I have a right to everything that relates to Violante. And he that traduces her fame, and refuses to give his reason for't, is a villain.                    [*Draws.*

*Col. B.* [*Aside.*] What the devil have I been doing? Now, blisters on my tongue by dozens.

*Fred.* [*Crosses.*] Pr'ythee, Felix, don't quarrel till you know for what; this is all a mistake, I'm positive.    [*Between them.*

*Col. B.* Look you, sir; that I dare draw my sword, I think will admit of no dispute. But though fighting's my trade, I'm not in love with it, and think it more honorable to decline this business than pursue it. This may be a mistake: however, I'll give you my honor never to have any affair, directly or indirectly, with Violante, provided she is your Violante; but if there should happen to be another of that name, I hope you will not engross all the Violantes in the kingdom.

*Fel.* [*Crosses.*] Your vanity has given me sufficient reason to believe I'm not mistaken. I'll not be imposed upon, sir.

*Col. B.* Nor I be bullied, sir.

*Fel.* Bullied! 'Sdeath, such another word, and I'll nail thee to the wall.

*Col. B.* Are you sure of that, Spaniard?           [*Draws.*

*Gibby.* [*Draws.*] Say na mair, mon. O' my saul, here's twa to twa. Ginna fear, sir, Gibby stonds by ye for the honor of Scotland.                        [*Vapors about.*

*Fred.* [*Crosses, comes down* C.] By St. Anthony, you sha'n't fight on bare suspicion; be certain of the injury, and then——

*Fel.* That I will this moment; and then, sir—I hope you are to be found——

*Col. B.* Whenever you please, sir.

[*Exit* FELIX *quickly.* COLONEL *goes up stage,* FREDERIC *trying to soothe him.*

*Gibby.* 'Sdeath, sir, there ne'er was a Scotsman yet that shamed to show his face. [*Struts about.*

*Fred.* So, quarrels spring up like mushrooms, in a minute. Violante and he were but just reconciled, and you have furnished him with fresh matter of falling out again; and I am certain, Colonel, Gibby is in the wrong.

*Gibby.* Gin I be, sir, the mon that tald me leed; and gin he did, I'll lick him as lang as I can haud a stick in my hond, now see ye.

*Col. B.* I am sorry for what I have said, for the lady's sake; but who could divine that she was his mistress? Pr'ythee, who is this warm spark?

*Fred.* He is the son of one of our grandees, named Don Lopez de Pimentell, a very honest gentleman, but somewhat passionate in what relates to his love. He is an only son, which may perhaps be one reason for indulging his passion.

*Col. B.* When parents have but one child, they either make a madman or a fool of him.

*Fred.* He is not the only child; he has a sister; but I think, through the severity of his father, who would have married her against her inclination, she has made her escape; and notwithstanding he has offered five hundred pounds, he can get no tidings of her.

*Col. B.* Ha! how long has she been missing?

*Fred.* Nay, but since last night, it seems.

*Col. B.* [*Aside.*] Last night? The very time!—How went she?

*Fred.* Nobody can tell: they conjecture through the window.

*Col. B.* This must be the lady I caught. [*Crosses* C.] Dear Frederic, I beg your pardon, but I had forgot I was to meet a gentleman upon business at five; I'll endeavor to despatch him, and wait on you again as soon as possible. [*Crosses* R.

*Fred.* Your humble servant, Colonel. [*Exit* L. I E.

*Col. B.* Gibby, I have no business with you at present.
[*Exit* L. H. I E.

*Gibby.* That's weel. Now will I gang and seek this loon, and gar him gang with me to Don Pedro's hoose. Gin he'll no gang of himself I'se gar him gang by the lug, sir. Gibby hates a lee. [*Exit* R. H. I E.

---

SCENE 2.—VIOLANTE'S *Apartment.*

*Enter* VIOLANTE *and* ISABELLA, D. L. U. E.

*Isa.* [R.] The hour draws on, Violante, and now my heart begins to fail me; but I resolve to venture, for all that.

*Vio.* [C.] What, does your courage sink, Isabella?

*Isa.* Only the force of resolution a little retreated; but I'll rally it again, for all that.

*Enter* FLORA, D. L. U. E.

*Flora.* Don Felix is coming up, madam.

*Isa.* My brother! which way shall I get out? Despatch him as soon as you can, dear Violante.

*Vio.* I will. [*Exit* D. R. H. I E. FLORA *exits* L.

*Enter* FELIX, *in a surly humor,* D. L. H. I E.; *throws himself sulkily into a chair.*

Felix, what brings you back so soon? did I not say to-morrow?

*Fel.* [*Aside.*] My passion chokes me; I cannot speak. O, I shall burst! [*Rises in agitation and sits again.*

*Vio.* Bless me, are you not well, my Felix?

*Fel.* Yes—no—I don't know what I am.

*Vio.* Heyday! what's the matter now! another jealous whim!

*Fel.* [*Aside.*] With what an air she carries it!

*Vio.* If I were in your place, Felix, I'd choose to stay at home when these fits of spleen are upon me, and not trouble such persons as are not obliged to bear with them.

[*Here he affects to be careless of her.*

51

*Fel.* I am very sensible, madam, of what you mean ; I disturb you, no doubt; but were I in a better humor, I should not incommode you less ; I am but too well convinced you could easily dispense with my visit.

*Vio.* When you behave yourself as you ought to do, no company so welcome ; but when you reserve me for your ill-nature, I waive your merit, and consider what's due to myself. And I must be so free to tell you, Felix, that these humors of yours will abate, if not absolutely destroy, the very principles of love.

*Fel.* [*Rises.*] And I must be so free to tell you, madam, that since you have made such ill returns to the respect that I have paid you, all you do shall be indifferent to me for the future ; and you shall find me abandon your empire with so little difficulty, that I'll convince the world that your chains are not so hard to break, as your vanity would tempt you to believe. I cannot brook the provocation you give.

*Vio.* This is not to be borne. Insolent ! You abandon ! You ! whom I've so often forbade ever to see me more ! Have you not fallen at my feet ? Implored my favor and forgiveness ? Did you not trembling wait, and wish, and sigh, and swear yourself into my heart ? Ungrateful man !—if my chains are so easily broke, as you pretend, then you are the silliest coxcomb living you did not break 'em long ago ; and I must think him capable of brooking anything, on whom such usage could make no impression.

*Fel.* I always believed, madam, my weakness was the greatest addition to your power : you would be less imperious, had my inclination been less forward to oblige you. You have, indeed, forbade me your sight, but your vanity even then assured you I would return, and I was fool enough to feed that vanity. Your eyes, with all their boasted charms, have acquired the greatest glory in conquering me. And the brightest passage of your life is, wounding this heart with such arms as pierce but few persons of my rank.

[*Walks about in a great passion.*

*Vio.* Matchless arrogance ! True, sir, I should have kept measures better with you, if the conquest had been worth preserving ; but we easily hazard what gives us no pain to lose. As for my eyes, you are mistaken if you think they have vanquished none but you ; there are men above your boasted rank, who have confessed their power, when their misfortune in pleasing you made them obtain such a disgraceful victory.

[*Up and down to face him.*

*Fel.* Yes, madam, I am no stranger to your victories.

[*Crosses* R.

*Vio.* And what you call the brightest passage of my life, is not the least glorious part of yours. [*Down* L.

*Fel.* Ha, ha ! don't put yourself in a passion, madam, for I assure you, after this day, I shall give you no trouble. You may meet your sparks on the Terriero de Passa, at four in the morning, without the least regard to me ; for when I quit your chamber, the world sha'n't bring me back.

*Vio.* I am so well pleased with your resolution, I don't care how soon you take your leave. But what you mean by the Terriero de Passa, at four in the morning, I can't guess.

[*They face each other.*

*Fel.* No, no, no, not you. You were not upon the Terriero de Passa at four this morning !

*Vio.* [*Crosses.*] No, I was not ; [*Shocked at her positive denial, he turns away with gesture of disgust. She continues, and speaks with firm resentment. She paces up and down. He follows her.*] but if I was, I hope I may walk where I please, and at what hour I please, without asking your leave.

*Fel.* O, doubtless, madam ! and you might meet Colonel Briton there, and afterward send your emissary to fetch him to your house—and upon your father's coming in, thrust him into your bed-chamber—without asking my leave. 'Tis no business of mine, if you are exposed among all the footmen in town—nay, if they ballad you, and cry you about at a halfpenny a piece—they may without my leave. [*Crosses to* L. H.

*Vio.* Audacious ! don't provoke me—don't ; my reputation is not to be sported with [*Going up to him.*] at this rate. No, sir, it is not. [*Bursts into tears. Aside.*] Inhuman Felix ! O, Isabella, what a train of ills thou hast brought on me !

[*Sits on sofa,* R.

*Fel.* [*Aside.*] Ha, now she's crying! I cannot bear to see her weep. A woman's tears are far more fatal than our swords. O, Violante. 'Sdeath! What a dog am I! Now have I no power to stir. Dost thou not know such a person as Colonel Briton? Pr'ythee tell me, didst not thou meet him at four this morning upon the Terriero de Passa?

*Vio.* Were it not to clear my fame, I would not answer thee, thou black ingrate! [*Rises.*] But I cannot bear to be reproached with what I even blush to think of, much less to act. By Heaven, I have not seen the Terriero de Passa this day.

*Fel.* Did not a Scotch footman attack you in the street neither, Violante?

*Vio.* Yes; but he mistook me for another, or he was drunk, I know not which.

*Fel.* [*Crosses* L.] And do you not know this Scotch colonel?

*Vio.* Pray ask me no more questions; this night shall clear my reputation, and leave you without excuse for your base suspicions. More than this I shall not satisfy you; therefore pray leave me. [*Crosses* R.

*Fel.* Didst thou ever love me, Violante?

*Vio.* I'll answer nothing. You were in haste to be gone just now; I should be very well pleased to be alone, sir.

[*Sits down on* R. H., *and turns aside.*

*Fel.* I shall not long interrupt your contemplation. [*Aside.*] Stubborn to the last.

*Vio.* [*Aside.*] Did ever woman involve herself as I have done?

*Fel.* [*Aside.*] Now would I give one of my eyes to be friends with her; for something whispers to my soul she is not guilty. [*Aloud.*] I'm going. [*Pause.*] I'm going. [*Pulls a chair, and sits by her at a little distance, looking at her some time without speaking; then he draws a little nearer to her.*] Give me your hand at parting, however, Violante, won't you? [*She draws her chair away, as he torments her with his feather. He follows her up, and finally lays his hand upon her knee.*] Won't you—won't you—won't you?

*Vio.* [*Half regarding him.*] Won't I do what?

*Fel.* You know what I would have, Violante. O my heart!

*Vio.* [*Smiles.*] I thought my chains were easily broke.

[*Lays her hand in his.*

*Fel.* [*Draws his chair close to her, and kisses her hand in a rapture.*] Too well thou knowest thy strength. O, my charming angel, my heart is all thy own! Forgive my hasty passion; 'tis the transport of a love sincere! O, Violante, Violante!

*Ped.* [*Without,* L. H.] Bid Sancho get a new wheel to the chariot, presently.

*Vio.* [*Down* C.] Bless me, my father returned!

*Fel.* Your father! The devil!

*Vio.* What shall we do 'now, Felix? We are ruined past redemption.

*Fel.* [R.] No, no, no, my love; I can leap from the closet window. [*Runs to the door,* R. H. I E., *where* ISABELLA *is, who closes it; noise of bolts heard within.*] Confusion! somebody bolts the door withinside. I'll see whom you have concealed here, if I die for't. O, Violante, hast thou again sacrificed me to my rival? [*Draws.*

*Vio.* By Heaven, thou hast no rival in my heart!—let that suffice. Nay, sure you will not let my father find you here. Distraction!

*Fel.* Indeed but I shall, except you command this door to be opened, and that way conceal me from his sight.

[*He struggles with her to come at the door.*

*Vio.* Hear me, Felix. Though I were sure the refusing what you ask would separate us forever, by all that's powerful you shall not enter here. Either you do love me, or you do not. Convince me by your obedience.

*Fel.* That's not the matter in debate. I will know who is in this closet, let the consequence be what it will. Nay, nay, nay, you strive in vain; I will go in.

*Vio.* You shall not go in.

*Enter* DON PEDRO, D. L. U. E.

*Ped.* Heyday! What's here to do? "I will go in," and "You sha'n't go in,"—and "I will go in." Why, who are you, sir?

*Fel.* [*Aside.*] 'Sdeath! What shall I say now?

*Ped.* Don Felix, pray what's your business in my house? Ha, sir?

*Vio.* O, sir, what miracle returned you home so soon? Some angel 'twas that brought my father back to succor the distressed. This ruffian—I cannot call him a gentleman—has committed such an uncommon rudeness, as the most profligate wretch would be ashamed to own. As I was at my devotions in my closet——

*Fel.* Devotions!

*Vio.* I heard a loud knocking at my door, mixed with a woman's voice, which seemed to imply she was in danger. I flew to the door with the utmost speed, where a lady, veiled, rushed in upon me, who, falling on her knees, begged my protection from a gentleman, who, she said, pursued her. I took compassion on her tears, and locked her in this closet; but, in the surprise, having left open the door, this very person whom you see, with his sword drawn, [FELIX *sheathes his sword*] ran in, protesting, if I refused to give her up to his revenge, he'd force the door.

*Fel.* [*Aside.*] What in the name of goodness does she mean to do?—hang me!

*Vio.* I strove with him till I was out of breath, and had you not come as you did, he must have entered. But he's in drink, I suppose, or he could not have been guilty of such an indecorum.                    [*Crosses* L.; *signs to* FELIX.

*Ped.* I'm amazed!

*Fel.* [*Aside.*] The devil never failed a woman at a pinch. What a tale has she formed in a minute! In drink, quotha! a good hint; I'll lay hold on't to bring myself off.

*Ped.* Fie, Don Felix! No sooner rid of one broil but you are commencing another. To assault a lady with a naked sword derogates much from the character of a gentleman, I assure you.

*Fel.* [*Counterfeits drunkenness.*] Who? I assault a lady! [*Crosses* C.] Upon honor the lady assaulted me, sir, and would have seized this body politic upon the king's highway. Let her come out and deny it if she can. Pray, sir, command the door to be opened, and let her prove me a liar if she knows how.

*Ped.* Ay, ay! who doubts it, sir? Open the door, Violante, and let the lady come out. Come, I warrant thee he sha'n't hurt her.

*Fel.* No, no, I won't hurt the dear creature. [*Aside.*] Now, which way will she come off?

*Vio.* Come forth, madam; none shall dare to touch your veil; I'll convey you out with safety, or lose my life. [*Aside.*] I hope she understands me. [*Noise of bolt heard*, R. H. I E.

*Enter* ISABELLA, *veiled.* VIOLANTE *leads her to* DON PEDRO, *who leads her off* L., FELIX *watching closely.*

*Fel.* [*Over* VIOLANTE'S *shoulder.*] Is it really a woman, though?

*Vio.* [*Laughing, but speaking low.*] Come and see. Get clear of my father, and return, when all mistakes shall be recti- fied. [*Exit*, D. L. H. I E. FELIX *offers to follow her.*

*Ped.* [*Draws his sword.*] Not a step, sir, till the lady be past your recovery; I never suffer the laws of hospitality to be violated in my house, sir. Come, sir, you and I will take a pipe and bottle together.

*Fel.* Damn your pipe and damn your bottle! I hate drink- ing and smoking.

*Ped.* [R.] First he will have a pipe and a bottle, and then he won't have a pipe and a bottle; and when I want a pipe and a bottle, he don't want a pipe and a bottle, and when I do want a pipe and a bottle, he doesn't want a pipe and a bottle.—As to smoking or drinking, you have your liberty; but you shall stay, sir.

*Fel.* [*Crosses* R.] But I won't stay; for I've been drinking Burgundy, and Champagne, and Imperial Tokay—I've been drinking Cham—[*This very joyous, then in maudlin tones.*]— but I love my own country better, and I don't like you. [*Very suddenly.*] And I won't stay—for I have the best reason in the world for my not staying.

*Ped.* Ay! What's that?

*Fel.* Why, I am going to be married; and so good-by.

*Ped.* To be married!—it can't be! Why, you are drunk, Felix.

*Fel.* Drunk! Ay, to be sure. You don't think I'd go to be married if I was sober. But drunk or sober, I am going to be married for all that; and if you won't believe me, to convince you, I'll show you the contract, old gentleman.

*Ped.* Ay, do; come, let's see this contract, then.

*Fel.* Yes, yes, I'll show you the contract, I'll show you the contract. Here, sir, here's the contract.

> [*Draws a pistol.* PEDRO *seizes a chair, and* FELIX *follows him around.*

*Ped.* [*Starts.*] Well, well, I'm convinced; go, go—pray go and be married, sir.

*Fel.* Yes, yes, I'll go—I'll go and be married; [*Going and then returning.*] but sha'n't we take a bottle first?

*Ped.* No, no; pray, dear sir, go and be married.

*Fel.* Very well, very well. [*Going, then returning.*] But I insist upon your taking one glass, though.

*Ped.* No, not now—some other time. Consider, the lady waits.

*Fel.* [*Aside.*] What a cross old fool! First he will, and then he won't; and then he will, and then he won't. But you'll take one glass.

*Ped.* [*Seizes a chair.*] Oh, go and get married.

*Fel.* All right, I'll go and get married. [*Exit.*

*Enter* VASQUEZ, D. L. U. E.

*Vasq.* Here's Don Lopez——

*Ped.* [*Not seeing who it is, picks up a chair and holds it before him.*] Go and get married—— Ah, it's you! Well?

*Vasq.* Here's Don Lopez de Pimentell, to wait on you, seignior.

*Ped.* What the devil does he want? He is not going to be married, too. Bring him up. [*Exit* VASQUEZ, D. L. H. I E.] He's in pursuit of his son, I suppose.

*Enter* DON LOPEZ, D. L. 1 E., *seen in by* VASQUEZ.

*Lop.* I am glad to find you at home, Don Pedro ; I was told that you was seen upon the road to —— this afternoon.

*Ped.* That might be, my lord. I had the misfortune to break the wheel of my chariot, which obliged me to return. What is your pleasure with me, my lord ?

*Lop.* I am informed that my daughter is in your house.

*Ped.* That's more than I know, my lord ; but here was your son just now, as drunk as an emperor.

*Lop.* My son drunk ! I never saw him in drink in my life. Where is he, pray, sir ?

*Ped.* Gone to be married.

*Lop.* Married ! To whom ? I don't know that he courted anybody.

*Ped.* [*Crosses* R.] Nay, I know nothing of that, but I'm sure he showed me the contract. Within there !

*Re-enter* VASQUEZ, D. L. 1 E.

Bid my daughter come hither ; she'll tell you another story, my lord.

*Vasq.* She's gone out in a chair, sir.

*Ped.* Out in a chair ! What do you mean, sir ?

*Vasq.* As I say, sir ; and Donna Isabella went in another just before her.

*Lop.* Isabella !

*Vasq.* And Don Felix followed in another. I overheard them all bid the chairs go to the Terriero de Passa. [*Voices heard outside.*] But I see they have all returned, for here is Donna Violante, and company with her.

*Enter* COLONEL BRITON, FELIX, ISABELLA, VIOLANTE, LIS-SARDO, *and* FLORA, R. H. 2 E.

*Lop.* So, have I found you, daughter ? Then you have not hanged yourself yet, I see.

*Col. B.* But she is married, my lord.

*Lop.* Married ! Zounds ! to whom ?

*Col. B.* Even to your humble servant, my lord. If you please to give us your blessing. [*Kneels.*

*Lop.* [*To* ISABELLA.] Why, harkye, mistress, are you really married ?

*Isa.* Really so, my lord.

[*Crosses with* COLONEL, *and both kneel to* LOPEZ.

*Lop.* [*To* COLONEL BRITON.] And who are you, sir ?

*Col. B.* An honest North Briton by birth, and a Colonel by commission, my lord.

*Ped.* She has played you a slippery trick, indeed, cousin. [*To* VIOLANTE.] Well, my girl, thou hast been to see thy friend married. Next week thou shalt have a better husband, my dear.

*Fel.* Next week is a little too soon, sir ; I hope to live longer than that.

*Ped.* What do you mean, sir ? You have not made a rib of my daughter, too, have you ?

*Vio.* Indeed, but he has, sir, I know not how ; but he took me in an unguarded minute, when my thoughts were not over strong for a nunnery, father.

*Lop.* Your daughter has played you a slippery trick, too, seignior.

*Ped.* But your son shall never be the better for't, my lord ; her twenty thousand pounds were left on certain conditions, and I'll not part with a shilling.

*Lop.* But we have a certain thing called law, shall make you do justice, sir.

*Ped.* Well, we'll try that ; my lord, much good may it do you with your daughter-in-law.

*Lop.* I wish you much joy of your rib. [*The old men go up.*


*Enter* FREDERIC, D. L. U. E.


*Fel.* Frederic, welcome ! I sent for thee to be partaker of my happiness ; and pray give me leave to introduce you to the

cause of it.  And now, my Violante, I shall proclaim thy
virtues to the world.

> Let us no more thy sex's conduct blame,
> Since thou'rt a proof to their eternal fame,
> That man has no advantage but the name.

*Vio.*  A few mistakes our sex may well excuse—
And this our plea no woman should refuse.
Your approbation, ladies, can't but move
The hearts of men which first you taught to love.
And they must applaud if you but favor,
And to success but give the savor.

CURTAIN.